FOOTPRINTS ON THE WATER

Footprints on the Water

Larry Tracey

Corryann Ltd

First published in Great Britain by Corryann Ltd in 2006

Corryann Ltd
1 Horseshoe Park
Pangbourne
Berks
RG8 7JW

www.corryann.com

Edited by
Lynne Summers

British Library Cataloguing-in Publication data
A catalogue record for this book is available from the British Library

ISBN 0-9551610-1-0

Typeset and Printed in Great Britain by Antony Rowe Ltd,
Bumpers Farm, Chippenham, Wiltshire

Monday
Nov 2010

Amy

Please let me know

   ... *to my family and friends who have helped me in this endeavour.*

your views on the ending!

Warm Regards

Larry

Prologue

Dresden – Germany, August 1992

KATYA struggled to raise her body from the ground. Yesterday's news... offers for old cars, new washing machines tumbled from her clothing as her legs pushed her upward through the tangle of yellowing newsprint.

Struggling to balance, first on her right foot, then on her left, she stood erect clutching a brown, paper bag to her chest. As her weight continued to shift from one foot to the other, Katya pushed the bag higher between her breasts until the neck of the bottle within touched her lips. She gulped fumes from the bottle. Casting it aside, she stumbled through the detritus around her feet.

The clothes that hung on her fleshless frame oozed stale urine and alcohol vomit, a cocktail of filth, the odour of decay. Katya stooped to pick up the front page of the newspaper which lay at her feet.

'BARCELONA OLYMPIC GLORY,' her lips silently mimed the last two words of the banner headline. Her fingers opened letting the paper slip past her stomach, past her knees, sliding over her ankles and feet.

Katya walked towards the sound of the approaching train. "Olympic Glory – Olympic Glory," she whispered as she stepped over the rails. Her feet, loose in old, laceless trainers, slipped on the rocks between the wooden sleepers. Katya Schmidt, twenty-eight years old, looked at the pale light coming towards her in the dawn. Her eyelids blocked out the light. She fell, her knees seeping blood on the crushed rocks, her head bouncing lightly on the silver rail.

Pain shrieked from metal wheels, the bite of the brakes on the inner rim at one with the muscles of the train driver, in spasm, strangling his bones. He had seen the figure step over the rail, turn towards him and fall. Now he waited, emergency brakes applied, tightness in his throat and chest, his legs braced. The distance between the figure and himself closed now more slowly and then became constant. His left foot slipped on the step as he raced from his cab. He picked himself up and ran to the body lying five metres in front of his engine.

. . . .

Katya could see the light through her eyelids. She opened her eyes. A nurse was talking to her, smiling. "Brother," she heard. Then Katya closed her eyes and lost consciousness.

Chapter 1

GERMAN DEMOCRATIC REPUBLIC
OCTOBER, 1975

KATYA lay in bed, snuggled under a patchwork quilt. Sunbeams cascaded into the bedroom through the window, past yellow curtains with imprints of blue forget- me-nots tied back by a sash on each side.

Katya smiled at the sunbeams. She squeezed Adie, her comfort, a knitted, woollen lamb, to her chest. Her eyes creased in delight as she anticipated her twelfth birthday. On the sixteenth of October, she was to have a party. Her friends, Helga, Sasha, Monika and Nadia would come. They would eat the sponge cake her mother would bake especially for them, so soft, jam and cream in the middle, the top dusted in fine sugar. They would drink lemonade and laugh at her father's jokes even though he had told them so often before. Then they would all sleep on the floor of her bedroom. With the door closed, they would talk through the night, giggling as they discussed the merits and faults of the boys of the village. Seven days to wait for her birthday mused Katya, squeezing Adie even tighter.

"Katya, hurry. You will be late for school," Heidi Schmidt called, interrupting her daughter's reverie. Katya leapt from her bed, poured water from the jug into the bowl, scooped two handfuls and splashed them onto her face. With a quick wipe of a towel, she leapt from her nightdress into her day dress, put a brush through her hair and then, pressing the wooden latch on her door, entered the living room.

Katya kissed her mother seated at the wooden table and sat beside her.

"You will need to leave in two minutes or you will be late," said Heidi, glancing at the clock on the wall as she poured a glass of milk for her daughter. Katya nodded her agreement, her mouth stuffed with the ham, cheese and bread from her plate. The wooden legs of the chair scraped against the wood floor as Katya rose, grasping the glass of milk. Heidi brushed Katya's hair as she swallowed the milk. Paul Schmidt pushed the door open, meeting his daughter as she handed the empty glass to her mother.

"Hi-bye," said Katya, quickly kissing her father's cheek as she passed him through the open door. Gently pushing her way through the goats gathered beside the wooden chalet, Katya gulped the crisp, mountain air. As she passed, she patted some of the goats on the head and then, clear of the goat herd, she lengthened her stride down the mountain path, the clinking and clanking of the bells worn by her father's goats fading as she increased her pace.

The song of the stream that she ran beside drowned out the last tinkle of the goats' bells. Leaves from trees and bushes bordering the stream fell into the rushing water, golden, red and brown surfers sweeping along on its surface. Katya focused on a red leaf as it passed. She stretched her stride to keep pace with the leaf. For almost two kilometres, she stayed alongside the leaf. Only two hundred metres to run to the bridge over the stream, then her path to school diverged from the tumbling water. Her lungs begged mercy; the ache in her left ribs cried enough. Katya pushed her legs to continue, only one hundred metres to the bridge, to the end of the race. The red leaf was now four to five metres in front. Katya pressed to close the distance. At the bridge, she stopped, hands on hips, mouth open, air sucked in, pushed out, almost no pause between. Katya's breathing slowed as she continued along the path through the meadow towards the schoolhouse. Her stride shortened, bouncing off the soft pads of her feet. She smiled. The red leaf had beaten her by ten metres.

Katya delighted in running. She could outpace all the girls of the village with ease. She expended only marginally more effort in outrunning the fastest of the boys. Her legs were long; she was as tall as Pieter, the tallest of the village boys. Katya lengthened her stride again as the sound of the school bell reached her.

Breathless, she bounded up three wooden steps and pressed the latch on the schoolhouse door. Inside, all of the other children were seated at their desks, five rows, six desks in each line. Katya sped to the empty chair behind the second desk in the second row.

Sylvia Mietl, the school ma'am, raised her head from the register on the table at the front of the class. She put down her pencil.

"Good morning Katya," she addressed the panting girl. "When you have your breath back, we will begin today's lessons," she said kindly, frowning at the boys sniggering in the fifth row.

The first lesson of the day was always Soviet Studies. Sylvia Mietl sighed quietly as she opened the required text published by the Communist Party. Her eyes raised from the book, looking sadly on the expectant faces of her pupils. She realised that the minds of her students were at their most receptive for the first lesson. It was the coupling of this knowledge with her abhorrence of all Communist doctrine that caused her sadness.

Sylvia's existence had been blighted by the consequences of State control. The State decided how people were to live, what literature they should read, what their minds should think, even who should live or die. Born in the village in 1917, Sylvia's childhood was passed in contentment. The youngest of three children, she had twin brothers four years older. Her father had been invalided from the Imperial Germany Army two years before she was born. His wounded, left leg had healed in a manner that caused him to limp slightly. The family lived from the fertile land of the valley, food never in short supply.

A Nationalist government was elected in 1936. Life in her valley continued much as before. She married Karl Mietl in the Spring of 1938. Within a year, he had been called to arms and died for his country in a training accident. All personal ambition had to be subsumed to the requirements of the State. Literature past and present was censured. Sylvia lived this doctrine through 1939, through 1940 when news of the deaths of her two brothers arrived. By 1945, the Nazis were defeated. Russian soldiers came to the valley, torched houses, killed her father, then her mother. Adolf Hitler's doctrine was now replaced with Joseph Stalin's.

Sylvia began to read from the prescribed text, aware that failure to do so would result in the termination of her teaching career. For over thirty years, she had concentrated on the future through her pupils as an antidote to the past.

Katya listened intently, determined to please Frau Mietl with her diligence.

The day's studies finished at four in the afternoon. Katya ran all the way back to the family chalet. She passed over the bridge, jogged alongside the stream, then sprinted the last two hundred metres up the incline to her home.

"Would you like to help bring the goats down?" her father asked the breathless girl. Katya bent over, hands on knees, nodded in response.

Paul Schmidt started to walk up the side of the valley

towards the higher pasture where the goats were grazing. Katya stood up and trotted after her father, grasping his right hand in her left hand when she caught up with him.

"How was school today?" asked Paul, gently squeezing his daughter's hand.

"Fine," replied Katya. "Helga and Sasha can definitely stay overnight for my birthday. Nadia is nearly sure. She should know by tomorrow. Monika's mother is not very well so she will have to wait. She wants to come but she doesn't want to leave her mother if she is still ill. I do hope she gets better quickly," finished Katya, struggling to contain her excitement.

Father and daughter turned their heads to smile at each other as they walked up the track to the higher meadow.

Heidi Schmidt stirred the bubbling pot on the stove. The wooden ladle in her hand pushed the ears of barley into the fragments of chicken meat, churning them with the carrots and turnips, patches of onion sticking to all. She could hear the bells approaching. It would not be long before Paul and Katya came in for their meal. Heidi moved the pot from the hot stove to the cooler side. She placed a white soup tureen beside the pot and ladled the contents from one to the other. Bowls, plates, spoons and knives were positioned in three neat settings on the green and white, check tablecloth which covered the pine dining-table. Heidi removed the two fresh-baked loaves from the oven, one for tonight's dinner, the other for breakfast and lunch tomorrow. Heidi's bread-baking routine was, almost always, a constant. The warm loaf, too soft to cut into slices, was diced into six large chunks.

Bread, butter, soup, utensils all sat waiting. Heidi surveyed her creation, wiping her hands on her apron in silent approval. Paul and Katya walked in. On seeing the laden table, they inhaled deeply through their nostrils.

Beaming smiles evidenced their conclusions. Katya was the first to enwrap her mother in a huge hug, then a noisy kiss on the cheek, lips compressed with intensity. Paul followed with a more gentle squeeze of his wife between his arms and a softer kiss on the crown of her head.

Life moved wondrously by for Katya. Monika's mother recovered so Monika was able to sleep over with Nadia, Helga and Sasha on Katya's birthday. Heidi Schmidt had knitted a chunky, blue, woollen cardigan with a goat-kid motif in white and brown on the back for Katya as a birthday present. Katya delighted in the gift. October passed. The sun hung lower in the sky, staying for less of the day. Naked trees became scrawny without their foliage. Seeds strewn about them were squirreled away to secret stores. Nature readied for bed, to slumber through the winter. Early December arrived. Wood cut in the summer was consumed by the fire that warmed the Schmidt's chalet throughout night and day. Paul sniffed the air and looked up towards the mountain peaks, shook his head and re-entered the chalet. "It's time to keep the goats off the mountain," he said.

That night, whilst they slept, the silent rain fell. Katya woke to the sound of stillness. Light waited outside her window as she drew back the yellow curtains though the sun was still to rise. The snows of winter had come, the uniform worn by all.

Katya was still able to go to school as less than ten centimetres of snow had fallen. Paul Schmidt finished strewing the hay in the goats' compound.

"Katya, I will come down to the village with you," he said, closing the gate of the corral.

Katya, her trousers tucked into her boots and her body wrapped in the treasured goat-kid cardigan, started to run. Powdered snow flew back in the face of Paul as he chased his daughter's footprints. Paul, one metre eighty-five tall, weighing roughly seventy kilograms, had been a champion mountain runner in his early twenties. Even today, aged thirty-three, he was the fastest man over distance in the valley. Paul was surprised at the effort he needed to catch Katya. They ran side by side, occasionally stumbling as they wandered from the path. Running through snow was better suited to the lighter Katya, Paul decided. This would explain the ache in his calf muscles, the tightening of his inner, lower thigh.

As they neared the schoolhouse on the edge of the village, Katya looked across into her father's eyes. Paul, recognising the challenge, conceded and decreased his pace. Katya sprinted, galloping knees high, the last two hundred metres to the school. Paul stopped to watch his daughter, his hands on his hips gripping his flesh between thumb and forefinger.

"I've been eating too well," he said to himself. "I need to cut back, exercise a bit more."

Chapter 2

WINTER passed. Katya missed some school on the days when the snow was too deep. Sylvia Mietl always gave her homework in all her curriculum subjects except Soviet Studies. Katya was conscientious, working six hours at home on each schoolday when she was unable to attend.

The snow had melted from the valley before the end of March. Tired, yellow-green grass in the valley meadows reacted with the snow-melt and the spring sunshine. Within weeks, the grass transformed into luscious, emerald-green blades pointing at the sun. By May, the blades of grass appeared outnumbered. White flowers, blue flowers, yellow flowers, pink flowers covered the meadows. On her run home from school, Katya stopped to pick a posy of yellow and blue flowers for these were her mother's favourites. She walked the rest of her journey, lightly holding the fragile stems. As she passed the stream, she saw a twig flowing on the surface being carried down the valley. Katya smiled. That morning, she had thrown a twig into the water and raced it for two kilometres, her final sprint taking her to the bridge a few seconds before the twig flowed under her.

Katya walked through the open door of the chalet. She handed the delicate flowers to her mother. Katya's face crinkled in bemusement. On the table, in the centre, was a sponge cake dusted in fine sugar, jam and cream oozing from the side separating the top from the bottom.

"Do we have visitors?" Katya asked.

"No," said Heidi, kissing Katya's puzzled cheek in thanks

as she took the posy of flowers from her. "We have some exciting news," said Heidi, arranging the flowers in an old jam-jar half-full of water. "The news concerns you but I would like us to share the moment with your father," Heidi said, looking for Katya's acquiescence. "I can tell you now if you wish," Heidi responded to the anxiety evident on Katya's face.

"No, no, I'm happy to wait and share the news," Katya replied, her body language in conflict with her words.

The tinkle of bells brought relief to Katya's face and a smile to her mother's. Katya and Heidi rushed out through the wedged-open door to share the news with Paul.

Surrounded by the goats, amidst an orchestra of clashing bells, Frau Schmidt told of the visit of Hans Kutz, the village mayor.

"Herr Kutz came to tell us that Katya has been selected to compete in the Regional Athletics Championships for girls under thirteen," maternal pride wrapped each word of Heidi's announcement.

Katya squeezed her eyes shut and clenched her teeth so that she could hold the news inside her head, all routes of escape being closed. Heidi and Paul Schmidt smiled, sharing in their daughter's joyous excitement. Katya came to her mother, left arm embracing her waist. Katya's right hand pulled her father closer so that she might hug both her parents in a family embrace. Heidi kissed the tears from her daughter's cheek as they spilled from Katya's open eyes.

Hugging abated, Heidi gently moved Katya's arm from her waist. "Time for your cake," she said.

Heidi and Katya munched on the sponge cake. Dabs of fine sugar clung to the tips of their noses. Paul sat, cake untouched on the plate before him.

"When is the race? What is the distance? How many

runners? Will there be heats?" His thoughts tumbled from his mouth as questions directed at the ceiling.

"The race is in six weeks. You will have to ask the Mayor or the athletics officials about the rest," responded Heidi, winking at her daughter in secret acknowledgement of Paul's excitement.

In the schoolroom the next morning, Sylvia Mietl announced the news to the class.

"One of you has been chosen to represent the district in the Regional Athletics Championships." The teacher paused in an attempt to add drama. The eyes of the whole class turned to Katya; they knew that in running, she was the best of them. "Katya Schmidt," said Sylvia, abandoning her attempt at suspense. Clapping and cheering from her classmates and her teacher pinkened Katya's cheeks. She felt the heat in her face. Her realisation that she was blushing increased its intensity.

Over supper that evening, Paul outlined a training programme for Katya. The plan was divided into running days and rest days. It was the method Paul had used when he ran in competition. He had made a few amendments to his old schedule such as lessening the distances covered on the running days as Katya was still only a young girl. Also, some of the running days were for sprinting only. Paul had spoken to the athletics officials. Katya's race would be 800 metres, only two laps. Katya would run in the second of three heats with eleven other girls of her age. The first four in each heat qualified for the final which would be run on the same day.

Katya listened intently as her father talked. She would enjoy the stamina training, running up the mountain. Especially, she looked forward to the training with her father who would run beside her.

The organised training improved Katya's pace. She could feel the extra power in her legs. On the rest days, she itched to train but had to make do with her daily school runs. When the rest day fell on a Saturday or Sunday with no school runs to absorb her energy, she pressed her father to let her run. Paul acquiesced with the condition that she run at half her normal pace. Katya found this rule hard to adhere to but kept to the spirit of it.

The day before race day arrived. Katya had been allowed to miss school. Paul had decided that the family should travel the day before, stay in a hotel overnight, then visit the stadium. Katya's excitement overpowered her; she could not sleep as thoughts of racing invaded her mind. Towards dawn, she finally managed to sleep for a few hours.

Saturday, race day, after a slice of bread and jam for breakfast, Katya, accompanied by her parents, walked from the hotel to the stadium. She was already wearing her running shorts and vest in the district colours. The district official had delivered them to the hotel the day before. White socks and black plimsolls completed her kit. She was ready to run. At the stadium, the district official met them, handed Katya's two competition numbers to Paul Schmidt with eight safety pins. Heidi pinned the numbers, back and front, on Katya's vest. Katya yawned, lack of sleep competing with excitement.

Race time, a kiss from her mother, a hug from her father, "Good luck," they said. Katya lined up in lane one alongside a girl two inches shorter. Each lane had two runners, a staggered start to be run in lanes for the first hundred metres.

"Get ready!" Bang! Katya surged forward, outpacing the girl beside her. The girls outside her, in lanes two to six, were in front of her so she increased her pace. She passed lanes two and three, catching lane four and then passing four and one of the girls in lane five before passing the other girl in lane five and both girls in lane six; now she was in front. When the stagger unwound, Katya was leading by fifteen metres. She led by forty metres as the bell rang for the final lap. Her legs felt tired; she pushed to run faster. Two hundred metres to go and she could hear the athletes behind her for the first time. At one hundred metres, her legs felt as though she was running up the mountain; one athlete passed her. Katya pushed her legs, her lungs burned. She tried to hold on but the girl in front was running away from her, breasting the white tape which broke, floating slowly to the ground. Katya pushed again, the line only five metres away. Another girl passed her on the inside, then another on the outside as she felt herself falling to the ground, gasping for air.

Paul Schmidt raised his daughter, held her under the armpits to assist her search for air.

"Sorreee, sorreee," Katya wheezed.

When Katya's breathing subsided, Paul lead her back to her mother.

"Well done," Heidi cried.

"You were fourth," said Paul. "You're in the final in six hours. You need to get some rest."

Katya's knees buckled; she slid to the ground, lying down on a grassy mound. Sleep came as the thought, "I'm in the final. I have another chance," ebbed from her mind.

Katya awoke four hours later. "How are you feeling?" her father asked.

"Much better now," Katya replied, her lungs and legs refreshed.

"Here, drink some orange juice," said Heidi, handing her a cup of orange cordial.

Katya took the cup, swallowing the contents. Heidi took the empty cup. "Here's a ham sandwich," she said, passing it to Katya. Heidi refilled the cup with orange squash and water. Katya ate the sandwich and drank the juice.

"I feel really good. How long before the final?" asked Katya.

"About ninety minutes. You need to do some jogging to warm up in an hour," replied her father.

The time for the final was close. Paul spoke to Katya after her warm-up.

"Don't run so fast at the start. Remember, there is a stagger. Keep in touch with number 349 in the mauve vest. She won your heat and your heat was the fastest heat so she's probably the fastest here."

Katya was again drawn in lane one. "Take your marks." Bang! The final was underway. Katya outpaced the girl beside her in lane one. Watching the girl in lane three, number 349, Katya held back as she ran the inside of the bend. She saw the girls in the outside lanes coming back to her. The stagger finished and all the athletes jostled gently into lane one. Katya moved into fifth place, immediately behind the mauve vest in fourth. Down the straight to complete the first lap, number 349 moved out into lane two, passing the three athletes in front as the bell rang. Katya tracked the mauve vest, her legs feeling strong. She bounced on the balls of her feet. With two hundred metres to go, Katya exploded. She lengthened her stride, increasing the power through her feet onto the track, passing number 349. Now in the straight, she ran faster still. The crowd screamed. She heard only silence as she broke the tape thirty metres in front of the second-placed mauve vest.

Katya trotted over to her parents, ears stretched back from the width of her smile. Heidi, sobbing, crushed her daughter in a fierce embrace. Paul gulped, his Adam's apple chasing up and down his throat as he fought to control his emotions, the effort unavailing as tears broke through his clenched eyelids, dripping down his sun-stained cheeks, shoulders juddering as his abdominal muscles shook his chest.

"Perfect, stunning," he cried, holding Katya gently by the shoulders. "How did it feel?" he asked, replacing his paternal delight with a coach's concern.

"Great. Much better than this morning. I...," Katya stopped as the district official clapped his hands firmly between her shoulder blades.

"Congratulations. You've made the National Championships," he said. Turning to Paul, he extended his right hand. "Well done, coach. The Nationals are in five weeks, in Berlin. The first two today have qualified. Presentations of medals are in thirty minutes." Releasing Paul's right hand, the official's left hand passed a plastic bag containing a new light-blue tracksuit to Katya. "Wear this for the award ceremony," he said, smiling at the open-mouthed girl holding the gift across her outstretched forearms.

At eleven thirty that evening, Paul and Heidi Schmidt stood in the doorway of their daughter's bedroom. Katya lay sleeping, Adie, her comfort, squeezed tight to her breast. On the table beside her lay the medal for first place; the light-blue tracksuit lay, neatly folded, on the chair. It was just twenty minutes since they had arrived home. Excitement, laced with exhaustion, had Katya in her bed within ten minutes, asleep within twelve.

Chapter 3

NEWS of Katya's victory passed mouth-to-mouth through the village. When Katya and her parents strolled down the main street, everyone either stopped them to congratulate her or shouted praise from across the street as they passed.

Monika, walking with her parents, squealed as she saw her friend walking towards her. She ran to meet Katya.

"You look great in that tracksuit," said Monika, exchanging kisses on the cheek with Katya. "Was this from yesterday?" she continued, now holding Katya by the shoulders, arms extended so that she might better view the new wardrobe.

"Yes," Katya replied, smiling at her friend's exuberance.

"Light-blue suits you," said Monika. "It matches the colour of your eyes," she finished, bear-hugging her friend.

Monika's parents caught up with their daughter and congratulated Katya. Then, kissing her cheek, Monika's mother hugged Heidi while Monika's father pumped Paul's hand.

"She may turn out to be more of a champion than you Paul," he chuckled.

"I think she already is," Paul replied, winking at Katya who was watching him over Monika's shoulder.

Progress down the street was slow. Monika had joined them, telling her parents she would be home by five. Having learnt the general detail of Katya's two races the previous day, Monika assumed the role of publicist.

"Cramps almost cost her a place in the final," Monika

told the Schenk family, bakers in the village, as they stopped to congratulate Katya and her parents.

"Katya, just pop in when you're passing. I'm sure there will always be a spare bun for you," Pieter Schenk, the baker, offered.

"The stitch made her stop; then she ran through the pain," Monika informed Hans Mandli, the butcher, as he shook hands with Katya.

"Mrs Schmidt, if you call in tomorrow, I will have a fresh pork chop to help Katya build herself up for the Nationals," the butcher offered.

"Katya vomited as she crossed the line," Monika related to Mrs Graf who stood with her husband, congratulating the Schmidts.

"Well, I'm sure some good spinach will give her more strength," Mrs Graf responded to Heidi Schmidt. Then, turning toward her husband, "Ulrich, make sure you set aside some good spinach for Heidi next time she's in the store. Katya will need the strength to represent the village in the National Championships." Ulrich Graf, the owner of the General Store, nodded in agreement with his wife's command.

Katya's celebrity stroll took almost ninety minutes as she walked the six hundred metres of the main street. Heidi turned to Paul, "We'd better start back if it's to take this long!" said Heidi.

"What would you like to do, Katya?" asked Paul.

Monika and Katya huddled, whispering. Katya replied cheekily, "Can Monika come and sleep over tonight?"

Paul looked towards Heidi. Tomorrow was Monday, a schoolday. Normally, he would refuse his daughter's request. Heidi shrugged, acceptance in her smile.

"Okay. Just this once," Paul replied, feigning sternness.

"You'll have to ask Monika's parents," Heidi said, smiling at the two girls.

Katya and Monika squealed, hugging each other in delight. Katya squeezed her mother, squashed her father.

Katya's bedroom door was closed. Past eleven o'clock that Sunday evening, whispers and giggling were evidence that the two friends were still awake. Heidi shook her head, chuckling to her husband as more laughter permeated the bedroom door.

"Sleepovers! There never seems to be much sleep. Talkovers would be a better description," she said.

Paul nodded, his thoughts elsewhere. "Katya will need to start her new training programme tomorrow," he replied, rising from his chair. "Time for us to get some sleep," Paul said and took his wife's hand, helping her to stand.

Katya and Monika had been late for school that Monday morning. They were late rising but, even then, they dawdled, talking all the way to the schoolhouse. Sylvia Mietl was cross when they arrived twenty minutes after the school bell.

"Winning running races is less important than your studies," she addressed the whole class to the crimson embarrassment of Katya.

That afternoon, Paul was waiting for Katya when she returned from school. He had brought the goats in early.

"We need to start your new training programme to prepare you for the Nationals," he said.

Katya nodded unenthusiastically, lack of sleep blunting her appetite.

"Are you sick?" he asked.

"No, no, just a little tired," Katya responded.

"Do you want to take today as a rest day and start the endurance running tomorrow?" Paul asked. Katya pondered the question.

"I'd rather get started. There's less than five weeks till I race," Katya said with conviction.

Paul outlined the new programme to Katya. "I've increased the endurance running. Now you will rest every third day. I think this will help with your base speed. We can work some more on your sprinting although I believe this is your strongest element." Paul spoke, Katya listened, excitement defying her tiredness.

Forty minutes later, Katya had completed the first day of the new training programme. She could not remember ever feeling so fatigued except, she corrected her memory, two days ago at the end of the first race. In bed at eight, she stretched her aching limbs, pulling the blanket around them. With Adie clasped to her breast, Katya's heavy head pressed into the pillow and she was asleep.

The next afternoon, Katya returned from school in buoyant mood. Sylvia Mietl had commended her performance in reaching the National finals. Revitalised by her twelve hour sleep, Katya was impatient to train. Paul was waiting when she arrived. He had decided to get up at dawn each morning, bring the goats to pasture and then take them down one hour earlier each training day afternoon. Paul jogged alongside Katya as they made their way across the meadow to the base of the hill they were to run up. Sprinting for fifty metres then jogging for fifty metres, they would run four sprints on the way up, improving strength from the incline. After a four minute rest, they would sprint four further bursts on the way down to increase leg speed.

Paul was comfortable on the uphill sprints. His extra power enabled him to keep pace with Katya and encourage her to push harder. "Sprint," he called at the next fifty metre marker. Paul had driven wooden stakes into the ground at fifty metre intervals when he paced the distance before the Regional race. "Jog," he called at the next marker, "Sprint," twenty seconds later. "Stop," he called as they reached the eighth stake.

Katya, hands on knees, gasped for air. Paul, blowing too, reached for his stopwatch hung around his neck and pressed the start button, four minutes rest before they started the downhill sprints, four minutes rest at the bottom before they started up again for the last time.

As he waited, recovering his breath, Paul turned the stopwatch in his hand. "NATIONALS, 1962, 2nd" was engraved on the back. He recalled the race, the five thousand metres men's final. A few weeks after his twentieth birthday, he had surprised the athletics experts with his performance. They were astonished that a youth could perform so well in an endurance event. Light boned, he was tall for a long-distance runner. His acceleration on the last lap had brought him through into second place, fifteen metres behind the winner.

Paul blinked at the memory, turned the watch to check the time elapsed. "Forty seconds to go," he called to Katya. Katya rose from her seat on the turf, ready for the downhill sprints. "Go," yelled Paul, pressing the button on his watch as the large hand passed sixty, the small hand, one tick away from the five.

Katya sped down the slope, her long legs stretching over the grass. Paul shouted, "Jog," as Katya passed the marker. He struggled to match her pace on the downhill sprints. He was unable to let his legs move as freely, always fearful that his head would overtake his toes.

Twenty minutes later, the training session ended. Katya and Paul jogged back to the chalet. "Go," Katya called, one hundred metres from home. Paul was already three metres behind when he started to pursue his fleeing daughter. "Beat you," Katya gasped as she touched the post on the goat corral which marked the end of the runs to home.

Katya absorbed her new training regime with ease. She always wanted to do more. Paul used this fact in his defence when Heidi fretted that he was pushing their daughter too hard.

School finished for the summer two weeks before the Nationals. The Regional official had visited them to go through the itinerary. He left a folder with Paul containing their train tickets to Berlin, their hotel vouchers, meal vouchers and authorisations for entry to the stadium.

"We'll be gone for four days. Who will look after the goats?" Heidi asked.

"Johann, Monika's older brother will come up and stay," replied Paul.

"All organised then. We're set to go," said Heidi with compressed excitement.

Chapter 4

KATYA entered the chalet carrying a jug of fresh goat's milk, bubbles still popping on the surface. She placed the jug at the centre of the table alongside a loaf of bread. She had been awake for over an hour, her feet sliding from her bed as the day's birdsong began. After breakfast, they would start their journey to Berlin.

Heidi came out of her bedroom. "I thought I heard the door," she said, kissing Katya on the cheek. Then, noticing the laden table, "Thank you for preparing breakfast," she said.

Breakfast over, Johann arrived to tend the goats. He had met Pieter Fischer with his pony and trap on the way to the Schmidt's chalet. Pieter offered the lad a free ride as he was going to collect the Schmidt family and their luggage.

Paul stacked their three small suitcases on the back of the trap. Pieter secured them with leather straps. Katya and Heidi, already seated, waved to Johann as the baggage handlers boarded. Johann waved back as the trap set off towards the train station in Kelstadt, ten kilometres distant.

Aboard the train, Katya sat next to the window, Heidi beside her, Paul opposite, facing them, cases stowed above their heads.

"Pieter wouldn't accept my payment," Paul said to Heidi.

"Why ever not?" asked Heidi, incredulously. She managed the family's finances with teutonic care.

"It's his contribution to Katya's challenge is all he would say," replied Paul. "I pressed him but he was determined."

The train lurched backward, then forward. Katya's arms, wrapped about herself, squeezed as her first ever train journey began.

Nose pressed to the window, Katya watched the fields, spotted with people, flick by. Now the track ran alongside a road, cars trailing behind them as the train sped on. A river flowed beside them and then left company, taking its own direction. The train approached a city. Single, charred walls of once noble buildings appeared on Katya's left-hand side of the train, modern, concrete plazas and statues of Soviet leaders on the right-hand side. The train halted at the city terminus and, fifteen minutes later, left the city of Dresden behind.

Katya's early rising, the rocking motion and the continuous clack, clack, clack, clack sound, combined to bring drowsiness. Katya's body twitched a couple of times as if it subconsciously felt it was falling off a chair. Then sleep came and stayed for four hours until they arrived in Berlin.

Their hotel was five minutes walk from the stadium. By the second day, Katya was accustomed to the broad streets, large buildings and the black exhaust from the gas-burning Trabants. Awe of the city was drowned out by the thoughts of her first race, tomorrow. The girl in the purple vest had introduced herself. Her name was Brigitte Meinhof. She and her parents would eat dinner with Katya, Heidi and Paul that evening as they were staying in the same hotel.

Brigitte was to run in a different heat to Katya. Over dinner, they chattered about the other girls that they had met at the track.

"There's no real form to go on," Paul addressed Mr. Meinhof.

"No, we will have more knowledge after tomorrow's heats," Mr. Meinhof concurred.

"What lane have you got?" Brigitte asked Katya.

24

"Lane six, on the outside," Katya replied. "What lane are you in?" she continued.

"Lane two," said Brigitte.

"I find the first hundred metres in lanes make pace judgement very difficult," said Katya.

"I have the same problem," said Brigitte.

"Time for sleep if you're to do your best," said Heidi, interrupting the two girls.

"You too, Brigitte. You'll need your rest," Mrs Meinhof patted her daughter's knee.

The two girls went to their rooms with mothers in attendance. The two fathers stayed to finish their beer and discuss training theories.

At the stadium, the next day, Katya watched Brigitte run twenty minutes before her own heat. It was not easy to discern the positions until the stagger unwound. Brigitte was then second. She passed the girl in front at the bell and opened up a twenty metre gap. Still clear coming round the last bend, it seemed she would win comfortably. Down the final straight, a girl in a green vest came storming past into second place, chasing Brigitte. The gap between them narrowed rapidly. Just before the line, Brigitte glanced round to see the green vest in her face. She lunged for the line, dipping her breasts to break the tape in front of her pursuer. Katya wiped her forehead with the fingers of her right hand. She wasn't sure how to interpret the result.

It was good that Brigitte had won as it meant that Katya was probably faster then the girls in that heat. Memories of being overtaken in the first heat of the Regionals when she had led too early were stirred by the late rush of the green vest.

"Katya, Katya, are you listening?" her father's words broke through Katya's thoughts.

"Sorry, what did you say?" replied Katya.

25

Paul held Katya's shoulders in his hands. "You're in lane six; you can watch all the girls on the inside. Adjust your pace if you think they are running faster. You need to be in the first four when the stagger finishes. Take the lead with two hundred metres to go. Your sprinting power should see you home," Paul said.

"Marks, set," Bang! Katya sped from the gun. The girl in lane five passed her. Katya ran harder; the girl in lane five responded. Katya matched her and looked across at the inside lanes. All the girls were running together in lane one. Bewildered they were in front, she suddenly realised she had missed the end of the stagger. She had run an extra bend, head to head with lane five. Katya crossed to lane one, lane five following her. The bell rang. Katya was twenty metres from the leader. She pressed, gaining ground. She had two hundred metres to go now and was on the shoulder of the leader but the effort to catch her had cost energy. Katya waited, staying on the leader's shoulder and recovered. At one hundred metres, on the last bend, the leader sprinted. Katya stayed behind, waited until the bend finished and then pulled out into lane two, lengthening her stride to burst into the lead, winning by ten metres.

That evening, Brigitte and her parents sat at the table in the corner for dinner. Katya and her family had found their own private alcove. Tomorrow, in the final, the two girls would be rivals. Katya ate well from the fixed menu.

"I'm too excited," she squeezed the words from her mouth, the last fragment of lettuce from her salad slipping from her lips and sticking to her chin.

"You'll be fine," said Heidi, dabbing the lettuce from Katya's chin with a white, paper napkin. "You won today even though you missed the finish of the stagger," she continued, cupping Katya's cheek in her left hand as she replaced the napkin on her knee with the other hand.

"It can be costly to be over confident," interjected a frowning Paul.

Katya and Heidi smiled conspiratorially, each patting the back of one of Paul's hands which he had placed either side of his plate. Paul's eyebrows expanded as the dual ministrations of his wife and daughter relaxed his face into a smile. The waitress arrived with the main course, a plate in each hand, a further plate balanced between the crook of her right elbow and the inside of her forearm. She placed a plate in front of each of the Schmidts. Katya tucked in. Pork, onion, dumplings and red cabbage combined to tighten her stomach.

Katya gave up half-way through a whole, stewed apple, fingers tapping on her drum-tight tummy.

"You've eaten really well," Heidi said, smiling at her daughter's charade.

"You'll need to be in bed early tonight," said Paul, accompanied by the screeching of his chair legs on the tiled floor as he pushed back from the table and stood up. "A walk outside to let the meal settle," he puffed, stopping to pick up the paper napkin that had fallen from his lap as he rose, "Will help us all," he finished, placing the crumpled napkin on his pudding plate. The Schmidt's left the restaurant exchanging nodded greetings with the seated Meinhofs as they passed their table.

They strolled the streets around their hotel looking in shop windows, watching the people descend from buses, queues of people waiting to take their places. Taxis with yellow lights crowning their cabs chugged by in all directions, street lights, neon lights, car lights adding to the luminary commotion. Paul, anxious not to get lost, had ensured that they walked only on the main street, two hundred metres up from their hotel. Up one side, down the other, now they were on the opposite side of the street to their hotel. "Right here," he said, directing his wife and daughter back to the haven of the hotel.

Katya clasped Adie, her comforter, to her breast. Her knees compressed the duvet held between them. Had she ever been this excited before? She thought not. Daylight shone through her window. Heidi and Paul were still asleep in the double bed beside her fold-away single. Katya rose and placed Adie on the pillow she had just puffed up. Holding the side of the duvet in her outstretched hands, she floated it down to lay flat, covering all of the bed except Adie and the pillow. Quietly, she gathered her day clothes, toothbrush and a towel, drew back the bolt on the door and walked the twenty paces along the corridor to the shared bathroom.

After washing, Katya dressed in her shorts, singlet, light-blue track suit and trainers and then opened the bathroom door. Her father stood in the corridor, waiting. They exchanged hugs as they passed.

"You're looking perky," said Paul as he stepped past. Heidi was up and dressed when Katya entered the room.

"I see you've made your bed already," she complimented her daughter. "As soon as I've washed, we can go down to breakfast," Heidi concluded, kissing her daughter's head as she left the room, washbag in hand.

Four hours later, Katya lay on her back sucking in air. Paul and Heidi rushed onto the stadium's grass infield to congratulate their daughter. Paul grasped Katya's hands and pulled her upright. Heidi hugged the new National Champion. Paul wept, his shoulders vibrating with emotion as he joined the hug, his smile wide enough to make any dentist content.

The Schmidts left Berlin by train the following morning. Paul smiled a troubled smile as his eyes rested upon his sleeping wife and daughter, their heads together resting on

Heidi's left shoulder. He closed his eyes, his tired body lulled by the motion of the train.

Pieter Fischer was waiting at Kelstadt station when their train arrived. He squeezed Katya's small hands within his own.

"We're all so proud, so proud that our village has raised a National Champion."

Katya grinned a happy response. The loaded pony and trap set off for the village.

"We have to stop at the schoolhouse. There is a reception in Katya's honour," Pieter spoke over his right shoulder to Heidi seated behind.

Almost the whole village was at the school to applaud them when they arrived. Compliments caressed their souls, Paul and Heidi as much the recipients as Katya. Herr Kutz, the Mayor, made a speech which rambled on. Sylvia Mietl rescued the shuffling audience.

"Cake and sandwiches are ready," she interrupted, pointing to a wooden, trestle table laden with food.

"Yes, yes, well, I had just finished," spluttered Herr Kutz, mindful of his dignity.

Katya's closest friends, Nadia, Helga, Monika and Sasha shared in her glory. The village boys offered their stuttered, embarrassed, congratulations to Katya, surrounded by her giggling girlfriends. The wash of joy had continued for almost two hours when Paul collected Heidi and Katya from the well-wishers.

"Pieter's waiting outside to take us home. I'm sure Johann will want to get to his own bed this evening, as will Pieter," he said, quietly shepherding his family out of the school-house, through the throng of celebrants.

Johann was waiting outside the chalet with his belongings when the pony trotted into the homestead. As Katya descended, he grabbed her by the waist and swung her

29

around. Her feet left the ground as he spun on his right heel. Paul grinned at his high spirits.

"Are the goats alright?" he asked.

"Yes, yes... no problems..." Johann panted, replacing Katya on her feet.

"Thank you for your help," said Paul, stepping towards the youth, open hand outstretched.

"We'd best be getting back," said Pieter as he placed the last suitcase on the ground beside him.

Johann bounded into the trap with his small case in his left hand. Paul shook Pieter's hand.

"Thank you, thank you," echoed Heidi and Katya. They stayed to wave until the trap was receding from view, then picked up their cases and re-entered their home.

Katya placed her new medal on her bedside table alongside the Regional Championship medal. In five minutes, she was snuggled under her familiar duvet, eyes wide open as she realised the pleasure she felt.

"I love this sooo.... much," she confided in Adie, squashing the woollen lamb between her budding breasts.

Chapter 5

IN the next room, Paul sat at the table, a glass of goat's milk in his hand.

"After the medal ceremony yesterday, I was introduced to Jurgen Klutch. He is the director of the National Institute for High Performance Athletes," he explained to Heidi.

"For what reason?" she asked.

Paul placed his milk on the table and held Heidi's hands in his own, "They want to coach Katya at the Institute."

"When? For how long?" replied Heidi, anxiously squeezing Paul's fingers.

"Early September. Then it will depend on how well she progresses."

"What does that mean?" countered Heidi, letting Paul's hands slide from hers.

"The Institute has been set up to identify and train potential Olympic Champions. So, if Katya stays in the programme, she could be there for more than ten years," Paul's voice hushed as he finished his judgement.

"But Katya's only twelve years old. It's still three months till she's a teenager. She's too young Paul," Heidi pleaded.

"I know.... I know. That is what I told him. Maybe in four years I said - when she's sixteen or seventeen."

"And what was the response?" she asked.

"He was not happy. He questioned my loyalty to the State. He said other parents had been proud to give up their children, honoured that they might bring glory to the State."

"Oh," Heidi exclaimed, her heart sinking.

"I told him I was a loyal Party member. I tried to compromise. I asked if Katya could stay at school here and attend summer training for the next four years. He said the system didn't work that way. He said the Institute had its own teachers to continue the schooling of its pupils. Katya would need to live in the Institute all year unless she failed to fulfil her athletic promise."

"What holidays would she have? How often could we visit her? How far away is the Institute?" the questions tumbled from Heidi's lips.

"I don't know. I didn't ask. I just said no. He told me to think it over and that someone will come to talk to us within the next few weeks." Heidi stood up and pulled Paul's head to her chest in soft embrace.

Three days later, they received a letter requesting their presence at the town hall in Kelstadt at 10 a.m. the following Tuesday. The letter stated that Katya's further education was to be discussed and that she should accompany her parents to the meeting. Paul's shoulders slumped as he passed the letter to Heidi.

"It is what we expected," she said as she finished reading. "I think we should discuss this with Herr Kutz to better understand the Party position. Then we should talk to Sylvia Mietl so that we have good educational arguments in our favour." She folded the letter and put it in her apron pocket.

"When shall we talk to Katya?" Paul asked.

"She's staying at Sashas's tonight, so when she returns tomorrow morning," Heidi replied. "We should try and see Herr Kutz and Sylvia Mietl this afternoon."

Herr Kutz greeted them politely. "Please take a seat Frau Schmidt, Herr Schmidt." He gestured to two chairs opposite to his own, a table between them serving as a desk. "How can I be of service?" he enquired.

Heidi handed him the folded letter. Herr Kutz unfolded

the letter, nodded and placed it on his desk. "I was informed of this in my official capacity," he stated.

"We are greatly honoured that our daughter may have the chance to bring glory to our country," Heidi flattered, "But Katya is only twelve; she is too young to leave home."

"She can train here with me," Paul interjected. "She has improved her times running up the mountains. She has won the Nationals. She could train in the summer at the Institute for the next three to four years, then go full-time."

"Yes, yes, what you say is possibly true but the Party needs your daughter," replied Herr Kutz. "Loyalty to the Party is paramount. Would you refuse their request?"

"Is there no discussion, no appeal to influence them?" Heidi implored.

"I believe not," Herr Kutz replied as he picked up the letter and handed it to Heidi, signalling the end of their meeting.

At the schoolhouse, Sylvia Mietl finished reading the letter.

"It says the meeting is to discuss Katya's further education," Heidi recalled. "They want to take her from us. She's only twelve. Who will help her into womanhood?" she sobbed.

Sylvia hugged the distraught mother, soothed her, quieted her.

"Would you be happier if Katya did not have her talent?"

Heidi and Paul looked at each other, probing into each other's souls. Sylvia looked on as they searched for the answer. She had no love of authority. The State had taken almost all that she had loved. Her teacher's instincts though, were to release talent, nurture and grow genius. Katya had a gift. Should a mother's and father's love stunt it?

"Running, running fast, faster is an important part of

Katya's spirit....but why must it take her from us?" Heidi replied.

Paul spoke, "We're proud of Katya and the talent she has. She should have the chance to see how far she can go, how fast she can be....but we simply wish that the authorities would compromise a little so that we don't lose her altogether."

"So, you would let Katya go but prefer if she were not away so long. Really, you'd like to see her as much as you possibly can," said Sylvia, summing up their thoughts. "How far is the Institute from here?" she asked.

"We're not sure," Paul replied.

"We will find out on Tuesday," said Heidi.

"Good luck. I will follow Katya's progress with an old teacher's pride in her pupil."

The following morning, Katya returned from her sleep-over at Sasha's. "Glass of milk?" Heidi asked as Katya slumped in an armchair.

"Okay," Katya replied.

"You look tired. Did you sleep at all?" asked Heidi, offering the milk-filled glass to her daughter.

"A bit," Katya replied, sipping the goat's milk.

"You've seemed tired since we came back from Berlin," Heidi continued.

"I'm not so much feeling tired as feeling empty," Katya responded.

"Empty, what's empty?" asked Paul as he walked through the doorway.

"Katya's feeling a bit low after the excitement of the Nationals," her mother explained.

"It is to be expected but it will pass. Once you have a new challenge, your spirits will rise again," Paul counselled.

"Maybe this is a good time to talk about next Tuesday?" said Heidi.

"What's happening on Tuesday?" Katya asked.

"You...." "Well" Paul and Heidi spoke simultaneously.

"Your mother will tell you," said Paul, deferring.

"Well, following your first place in the Nationals, you have been invited to attend the National Institute for High Performance Athletes."

"Wow, that's great," whooped Katya. "What does it mean?"

"It means you will attend the Institute full-time to see if you have Olympic potential. They will provide school lessons also. You could be there for ten years if you do well," Heidi replied. "It does mean that you will have to board at the Institute as it's not near here but we would see you as often as we can and you would be able to come home from time to time."

"Fan...tastic!" Katya shrieked.

"We will miss you but it's such a great opportunity and one day, maybe one day, it will mean you might stand on the podium at the Olympic Games to receive a medal," said Heidi, smiling with a heart full of sorrow.

"Oh, Mama, it would be wonderful but I would be so sad to be away from you," Katya responded, rising to cuddle her mother. "I'll be back to see you as often as I can.... and my friends," she said in an effort to comfort.

"I'm pleased you're so happy," said Paul. "We have to go to Kelstadt on Tuesday morning to sort out the details."

That night, Katya cried and cried until the emotion fatigued her into sleep. She loved her life, her room, her parents, the goats, the valley, her friends, the village. She cried because she knew she would miss them. In her quest to see how fast she could run, she would miss them. How good might she be? Could she be the best, the fastest in the world? Could she be the Olympic Champion? Others obviously thought she had the potential. The Institute would answer these questions. Then her mind turned again to not waking up in her own bed, not seeing her mother, not eating at her table, not running in the mountains with her father. Tears flowed. She turned the pillow in search of a dry patch.

Chapter 6

EARLY SEPTEMBER, 1976

THE carriages collided, each smacking into the buffers of the one in front and then ricocheting as the train braked alongside platform twelve at Dresden station. Paul tipped forward onto his toes, then rocked backwards onto his heels as he stood with Katya's cases, one in each hand. Katya opened the carriage door and descended. Heidi followed, clutching a wicker basket of baked goodies. Paul stepped down sideways carrying the luggage.

The taxi from the station took forty minutes to drive the twenty kilometres to the Institute's campus, south of the city.

Katya was taken to the dormitory room that she would share with eleven fellow female athletes. A porter had taken her cases from the taxi. Paul and Heidi had hugged, kissed and hugged again their goodbyes. Heidi had passed the basket of cakes to her daughter, stoically holding back her tears.

"See you in thirteen weeks," she had smiled at her daughter.

The taxi had left with her parents. Heidi had waved until they were gone from view, sadness and elation in her heart.

One other girl was in the dormitory when Katya flopped on the bed allocated to her.

"Hi, my name is Helga," she introduced herself.

"Hi, I'm Katya."

"You've missed lunch but dinner is at six," Helga said as the porter arrived with Katya's cases. "Would you like some help unpacking?" Helga offered.

"Thank you," Katya responded. "How long have you been here?" she enquired.

"About four hours longer than you," Helga replied, "But I have looked around and so I know a little of the layout, the canteen, the showers, the toilets. There is an official tour of the facilities tomorrow afternoon at three p.m. Most of the other girls will have arrived by then."

Katya took the cotton towel from the top of the wicker basket. "Would you like a piece of sponge cake? It's really good," she said, pushing the basket toward Helga who had sat on the end of Katya's bed.

"Mmm . . . . looks delicious," Helga responded, dipping her fingers into the basket and plucking out a slice of jam sponge sandwich. She moved it gingerly toward her mouth.

"Yum . . . me," she warbled, licking crumbs from the edges of her mouth. "Did you bake this?"

"No, no. I'm no sort of cook. My mother baked it," Katya laughed.

"I'll just finish this, then I can show you around, well, as much as I've discovered since this morning."

"I'd like to unpack first if you don't mind," Katya replied.

By the end of her seventh day at the Institute, Katya slept through the night without sobbing for the first time. It helped that the other girls in the dormitory were also adjusting to life away from home as the effect of noisy sorrow was contagious. Katya was comforted by the company of Brigitte Meinhof who was billeted beside her. They each lay on their beds, resting on their elbows, cupping their chins between their hands.

"What's your opinion of Alex?" Brigitte asked.

"Alex, Alex who?" Katya responded with lowered eyebrows.

"Our coach silly, Alex Durnek," Brigitte retorted.

"Oh, I haven't been permitted to use his Christian name. He obviously favours you," said Katya, grinning.

"Well, I need his help more than you do. You beat me by eight seconds at the Nationals. That's twice I've been second behind you. I want to beat you. Alex will help me improve. So, what do you think of him?"

"Actually, he scares me a bit. I try to do what he asks because I want him to be satisfied with what I do but I'm not sure that I'm succeeding," Katya replied, clambering off her bed. "We need to go. We have lessons in ten minutes," she said, looking up at the clock attached to the wall opposite.

As the months passed, Katya became more relaxed when training with Alex. He seemed less formidable to her as she improved her understanding of his body language. A slight nod of the head was a signal of congratulations, silence meant he was satisfied and a raised left eyebrow was a semaphore for more effort. During breaks in training, he occasionally shared their table in the café, displaying a wry sense of humour.

A week before Christmas, the girls were allowed home-leave of four weeks.

Katya pushed open the door of the chalet and inhaled the familiar piquancy of her home. The table was set, fresh bread, honey, goat's milk in the blue jug and a sugar-dusted sponge cake it's ornaments. Heidi beamed, crushing her daughter's head against her breasts. Tears rolled down her cheeks, wetting Katya's hair beneath. Katya felt the throb of the sobs through her mother's breasts and she cried too. Paul carried Katya's case to her bedroom, pride and joy swelling his chest as he passed the embracing women.

Christmas passed as did Sylvester (New Year's Eve), one

week later. Friends came to visit and Katya visited them in their homes. She luxuriated in the exquisite pleasure of being with those she held closest, her parents and her friends. She also delighted in the pleasure of sleeping in her own bed. Moments and memories, commonplace before, now were sensually heightened by her absence.

Two weeks into the New Year, it was time to leave. Paul and Heidi travelled with her to the train station, choked their goodbyes and waved as the locomotive took her away.

For the next month, Katya sobbed each evening. The pain of being away from home would not abate. Her coach, Alex Durnek, noticed the sadness in her.

"Katya, are your teeth rotten? Is that why you no longer smile?"

"No, Herr Durnek," Katya responded, smiling at his analysis.

"You should call me Alex. Since you returned from leave, you have been less happy. Do you have troubles at home?" he asked.

"No....not exactly......It's just that I miss it so much....," Katya sobbed.

"Then you should go home now. Pack your bag and go. I will take you to the station," Alex stated.

"But......but......my training......"

"Yes, you will miss your training and you will lose your place at the Institute but it is not a prison. You can leave if you wish."

"I want to train; I want to become a champion. I just miss home."

"Ah, so you want two things and each excludes the other. Katya, it's your choice. To become a champion, and I believe you can become a champion, you cannot live at home. So, go and think about which you want most and we will talk again tomorrow."

"No Herr... Alex. I know what I wish for. I want to be a champion runner. I need to know if it's within me," Katya said, responding both to Alex and herself.

"Good, good. Now you have made this decision, I think that you will accept being away from your family and friends more readily. So, are you ready to go to the track?" he said.

"Yes, I'm ready," Katya replied with a grin.

Chapter 7

KATYA, now reconciled to her ambition, settled into her training routine. Each Saturday, she wrote a letter to Heidi and Paul detailing her week's activities.

Dear Mama and Papa,

It is frosty outside but we have very good heating so I am writing in my vest and shorts. Sometimes the heating is too strong at night and I do not sleep well. We had roast pork on Wednesday evening with dumplings. I think we are having deer for lunch tomorrow. Last time we had deer, they gave us some amazing, sweet-flavoured cabbage. It was a great meal so I am looking forward to tomorrow.

My hair is quite long. I was going to have it cut before Christmas but I didn't. What do you think? How much should I have cut off? Brigitte thinks it looks better long but she has cut her own hair very short. I think I can run faster if it's short. My times are improving and Alex seems quite pleased. We have an assessment at the end of this month so I want to do really well. Perhaps I will cut my hair as short as Brigitte's. It seems to be the fashion now.

How is everything at home? I got your last letter on Wednesday. Thank you. I was sorry to hear that Frau Mietl has been unwell. Please give her my best wishes and tell her I will visit the next time I am home. Mama, you should give her some of your milk and honey medicine to make her better. Get the milk from Matilda as I am sure she produces the sweetest tasting goat's milk in the valley. Papa, you asked about my school lessons. I am trying hard to study as well as train and my marks are quite good really.

We had a bit of a scare on Monday night. The fire alarm sounded at two in the morning and we all had to leave our dormitories and stand outside, just in our nightdresses, for nearly an hour. We all huddled close together to try to keep warm but there was no fire. Someone had set the alarm off as a prank. The Direktor was not impressed. A new notice was posted on the board on Tuesday threatening expulsion for anyone caught tampering with the alarm system.

Well, I think I will get some scissors and cut my hair now. No, I will wait until you tell me what you think. I hope you are both well and the goats, especially Matilda. Mama, don't forget your medicine for Frau Mietl. I will look forward to receiving your next letter.

Your loving daughter, Katya
xxx

Katya patted the letter on the blotting paper pad, folded it across the middle and slid it into the envelope. She licked the gum on the inside flap, creasing her face in distaste. Flipping the envelope over, she wrote her family address on the front and then tamped the wet ink on the blotter, adding to the hieroglyphic patterns as Brigitte walked into the library.

"Are you busy?" she asked.

"No, I've just finished a letter to home," replied Katya.

"Ouch.... I must write to my parents soon," Brigitte

said, "Would you like to come for a walk to the town?" she continued.

"Sure. Are we leaving right now?" asked Katya, glancing at the large wall-clock.

"Whenever you're ready," responded Brigitte.

"Training starts at two thirty so we should be back in plenty of time," said Katya.

"Hopefully, we'll be back for lunch at one o'clock," said Brigitte.

"Well, that gives us two hours so let's go," said Katya, popping her letter into the pine post box on the table by the door.

The two girls giggled their way into town. Amusement was provided by verbal caricatures of the staff at the Institute, interspersed with feigned aloofness at wolf whistles from boys they passed on the road.

"He was quite good-looking," Katya whispered, turning her head to look back at the latest boy they had ignored.

"Only if you can forgive the acne," chortled Brigitte. "I fancied the tall, blonde haired boy on the bicycle," she said.

"Ugh! . . . Too skinny and his face is too long," responded Katya.

They arrived at the café in town just before midday.

"Let's have a soda and then we'll need to start back," suggested Katya.

The walk back was much quicker. There were less boys to distract them and their stomachs influenced the cadence in their footsteps.

At two fifteen, Brigitte and Katya were at the training track waiting for Alex. He arrived, five minutes later, clipboard in hand and a small aluminium stopwatch on the end of a cord necklace jiggling against his track suit top.

At four o'clock, he nodded his last affirmation of satisfaction for the session.

"Tomorrow, I would like you to run an eight hundred metre time trial," he said, addressing both girls. "Oh and I would also like you to meet my wife and baby daughter. My younger sister is staying with us so please come to our apartment for tea at five tomorrow afternoon," he concluded as he left.

"Wow and wow again," Brigitte squealed. "We'll see his baby AND I can see if I've closed the eight second distance between us."

"I'm looking forward to holding their baby but I'm a bit nervous about racing you," Katya said, pretending to quiver with fear.

"I'm definitely quicker than I was last year," said Brigitte.

"Well, we will know tomorrow," declared Katya. "Let's go and shower before tea," she said, clasping Brigitte's right shoulder in a comradely hug.

Katya sat on the sofa, the vee between her thumbs and forefingers supporting the nine month old armpits of Anna Durnek. The baby's feet danced upon Katya's thighs as she raised and lowered the infant. Bubbles of wet delight gurgled from Anna's mouth as she watched her reflection in Katya's sparkling, blue eyes.

"Teresa is training also. Soon she will be a qualified nurse," Alex boasted. His younger sister smiled at her brother's pride in her.

"It seems you have found a good babysitter," Teresa smiling, addressed Mika his wife.

"This is a great apartment," Brigitte interjected.

"Yes, thank you," Mika replied. "We have two bedrooms so Anna has her own room. Alex's job entitles us to special consideration. We can even shop in the restricted store and Anna will be able to have the best education," Mika continued proudly. "Alex has earned it. He had to work very hard. He scored the highest marks at the National Institute for Sports Culture in his year."

45

"Now, enough of me," Alex interrupted. "Well done on your time trial today. They have both improved their best times by almost four seconds," he said, addressing his wife.

"Would you like some more lemonade either of you?" Mika asked, picking up the half-full jug from the table.

"No, thank you."

"Yes, please."

Katya's answer preceded Brigitte's as she continued to bounce the baby's feet upon her thighs.

That evening, as they lay on their mattresses, Katya turned to Brigitte in the adjacent bed, "I liked Mika Durnek."

"Yes, but I think you liked the baby more. I hardly had any time to cuddle her," Brigitte replied.

"Sorry. Were you pleased with your new personal best time this afternoon?" Katya said, changing the subject.

"Sort of. I was happy to bring my time down by four seconds but you did the same so I am still eight seconds slower than you," Brigitte pouted.

"If we keep training, I am sure we will both run much faster by the time we are seniors," Katya speculated.

"Mmm......," Brigitte sighed, unconvinced.

On Thursday morning, after breakfast, Katya made her daily check of her mail slot. Nestled in the wooden slipper under her name was a letter from her parents. Elated, she tucked the letter into her maths book to read at the mid-morning break.

After her maths lesson, Katya sought out the quietest corner of the library to read her missive from home. She inserted her little finger into the corner of the envelope flap and ran it along the length until the sheet inside was exposed. She pulled it out. Most of the handwriting, she recognised as her mother's with a postscript note at the bottom written by her father.

Dear Katya,

I hope your lessons are going well and that you are getting good marks. It is really important that you eat and sleep properly to stay attentive to your teachers. Your old teacher, Frau Mietl, is much better and is back at school.

I met Monika in the butcher's yesterday. She was buying pork sausages. Well, that's what her mother asked her to buy but Herr Mandli only had beef. By the way, he asked me to pass on his best wishes to you. So, where was I, oh yes, Monika's mother is with child so Monika was doing the shopping. Anyway, I told her beef would be just as good as pork. She asked me to send you hugs and kisses but I told her she could write to you herself. She said she'd wait and see you when you come over next.

This letter is a day later than usual but that's because I went to see my brother Wolfgang yesterday. He sends his best wishes too. Your father has just come in with your letter so I will read it before I write anymore.

Your suggestion of milk and honey for Sylvia Mietl could work. I know she's better but it always takes time to recover fully. I will get some of Matilda's milk this evening. Your hair was just the right length when you were home. If you feel you need to cut it, please don't be too severe. Your father wants to write something so I will pass him the letter now. I hope you are happy, eating well, studying hard, making friends and running faster. Can't wait to see you at home again.

Love Mama
xxxxxxx

Dear Katya,

*I am pleased your marks are good. Well done. I hope the
training is improving your speed. I look forward to your next
visit home. The goats are all well.*

Love Papa
Xxx

Katya folded the letter and slid it back into the envelope.
Back in the dormitory, she would pin it within the elastic
band which held all her post from home.

Chapter 8

OVER the next twenty-four months, Katya absorbed her new routine, training with Alex, studying, home visits. The earlier sadness abated. She had accepted the personal cost of striving to become a champion. Her running was faster; she had belief in Alex and his programme.

Brigitte stopped training with Katya in 1979. Her timing had improved but only at the same rate as Katya so the gap between them remained. Brigitte was allocated a new coach, Dieter Muller.

Throughout the spring and summer of seventy-nine, the two friends trained apart but otherwise enjoyed each other's company. The training sessions were longer now as was the ensuing fatigue in Katya's muscles. Alex coaxed and cajoled her.

"It's natural you should feel tired with the increase in the training load. Your body will adjust. Your times are still improving."

"Brigitte told me she is being given vitamin tablets to help her," Katya responded.

"It's not necessary for you. You eat well. The canteen offers a good variety of food...."

"But," Katya interrupted, "Maybe the vitamins...."

"No......," Alex interjected. "You should not take them. They are not good for you," he said sternly.

Katya accepted Alex's judgement. She reduced the amount of time spent on schoolwork and increased her friendship with her pillow to ease her aching muscles.

On the 18th August, 1979, Alex was summoned to present himself in the Direktor of the Institute's office at three p.m.

Alex arrived in the ante-room at five to three. Five minutes later, the Direktor's secretary, responding to a buzzing, red light on her desk, ushered Alex into the Direktor's office. The Direktor, seated behind his desk, pointed at a chair.

"Please sit, Herr Durnek," he said, opening a file. Alex sat, placing his own file upon his knees.

"As you know, I have called you here today to review the performances of one of your athletes, Katya Schmidt." The Direktor looked up from his file, eyes now fixed on his inferior. Alex mutely declined the unspoken offer to speak.

"So, I have her times for each of the past three years. Please give your assessment of her progress," the Direktor instructed.

Alex opened his file and took out twenty-two sheets of handwritten forms.

"When Katya came here, her time for eight hundred metres was two minutes forty-five point six seconds. In her second trial, on the 12th December, 1976, she improved by one point three seconds. In her third ... "

"Herr Durnek," the Direktor said sharply, "I do not want a report of each of her time trials over the past three years. I have that data here," he said, letting the heel of his right hand strike the folder in front of him. "What is her current performance and rate of improvement?"

Alex turned to the top sheet in his file. "Her last trial, as you know, was two minutes nineteen point eight seconds. This indicates that she is on course to run eight hundred metres inside two minutes before the Los Angeles Olympics in 1984. I believe, however, that she has the endurance to be more competitive over longer distances. fifteen hundred metres or, the new women's Olympic event, the three thousand metres steeplechase."

Alex paused as the Direktor wrote notes in his folder. When he had finished writing, the Direktor pointed his nibbed pen at Alex.

"Herr Durnek, how do you explain your athlete being beaten by Brigitte Meinhof in the last trial? Until six months ago, Schmidt was consistently eight seconds faster than Meinhof. Now, Herr Muller's athlete is quicker...." Alex waited. "I'll tell you why, Herr Durnek. It's because Herr Muller gives his athletes vitamin supplements and thus far, you have refused to do so. This cannot...."

"They are not vitamins. They are illegal drugs....," said Alex, quietly interrupting.

"Oral Turinabol is not an illegal drug," shouted the Direktor. "It is a scientifically proven supplement to aid muscle recovery, approved by the National Sports Medical Service."

"That is not true," said Alex. "It is an anabolic steroid. There is no science to support its use. You are experimenting and using these young girls as laboratory animals," Alex challenged. "I will not administer poisons to my athletes," he concluded.

"Herr Durnek, you should be more careful with your words. The State police might consider them subversive. Our programme is approved at the highest level. We have a national duty to perform. It is my duty to report your outburst to the relevant authorities," he said, scolding Alex who remained silent. "However....," continued the Direktor, interpreting Alex's silence as acquiescence, "You come here with exemplary grades from the Coaching Institute and have performed well these past four years. Put Katya Schmidt on the drugs when she returns from her summer break and I will recommend that today's nonsense is not written in your record," he said, conciliatorily.

"No. I will not," replied Alex, standing.

"Herr Durnek," exploded the Director, "It reflects badly on my reputation to have such subversive elements in my Institute. You have one hour," he said, looking at his watch. "If you do not agree to obey my direct orders by four forty, you are finished. Talk to your wife because you will lose every privilege you have. Sixty minutes, Herr Durnek. Now go," said the Direktor, dismissing his subordinate.

Alex's body trembled uncontrollably as he walked towards his apartment. Mika knew when Alex opened the apartment door that the meeting with the Direktor had gone badly. She carried the sleeping baby resting on her shoulder and placed her in her cot. Alex was seated on the sofa when she returned. Mika sat next to him and nestled his hands between her own palms.

"How bad?" she asked.

"I must destroy the lives of children," Alex answered, thoughtfully. "Either I poison my athletes with no real understanding of the side-effects or I lose the means to feed our child."

"We'll lose the apartment, Anna's education, all that we have strived for, everything," Mika mouthed, stunned at the import of her words.

"Yes, everything," replied Alex. "I could even go to prison if the State police get involved."

"No, no," Mika implored.

Alex clasped her head and held it gently against his beating heart.

"Mika, I want two things and each excludes the other. The price is high whichever I choose. I don't know exactly what the cost is to us if I leave. We will definitely lose all the benefits but there will be more penalties that I cannot yet imagine. To stay, I must poison my athletes, destroy their young bodies for the glory of the State. This, I know, is a price too high."

"But even if you go.... someone else will poison them.... You leaving won't change anything....except for us....," sobbed Mika.

Alex held Mika's head. His palms pressed against her cheeks. He looked into her tear-filled eyes.

"Mika... I love you... If we stay, I would no longer love myself. I do not believe you would still love me or even yourself," the last word was squashed from his mouth as Mika crushed his lips against her own.

Chapter 9

EARLY SEPTEMBER, 1979

KATYA returned to the Institute and was introduced to her new coach, Dieter Muller. He introduced her to the pink and blue vitamin pills which he said would help her with her training fatigue. Katya was pleased; she was now training harder and for longer but not suffering the tiredness she had endured when Alex coached her. By the summer of 1980, she had improved her best time by nine seconds. Brigitte improved her time by five seconds and was now having injections as well as her pills. By the summer of 1981, Katya had reduced her best time by a further three seconds. Brigitte ran eight hundred metres in one minute fifty five seconds at the Institute on her eighteenth birthday. During the season, she had reduced her personal best by twenty seconds to become, unofficially, the fastest woman in the world that year, thirteen seconds faster than Katya. Four weeks after her birthday, eighteen year old Brigitte Meinhof died of heart failure, the third girl at the Institute to die suddenly that year. On instruction from the Sports Medicine Service, the Direktor reduced the injected doses of testosterone by ninety per cent. Dieter Muller congratulated himself that, of his athletes, only Brigitte and not Katya, had been on the intensive testosterone programme.

In the spring of 1982, Katya's training programme was changed. The Direktor wanted her to experiment with longer distances of fifteen hundred metres and the three thousand metre steeplechase. As she passed through her late teenage years into her early twenties, Katya became increasingly introverted. She never replaced Brigitte as her best friend and confidante. Letters home became less frequent, shorter, relating only to her progress in running and the opinions of her coach, Dieter.

23rd March, 1984

Dear Mama and Papa,

I ran the 3000 metre steeplechase in nine minutes ten seconds today. Dieter says I have a good prospect of representing the D.D.R. in the Olympics in Los Angeles this summer. He says I have a good prospect for the gold medal.

Hope you are well.

Your daughter,
Katya x

Katya's ambitions for gold in 1984 were quashed when the Deutsche Democratic Republic mimicked Russia in boycotting the Los Angeles Olympics. Katya stayed at the Institute throughout that summer, now with her own bedroom, training with Dieter. Paul and Heidi were disappointed that she would not race in the Olympics, saddened that she was to stay at the Institute during her normal summer break.

"She's changed so much these past few years," Heidi addressed Paul as they sat on a bench outside the chalet, watching the shuffling goats tinkle as the bells about their necks clashed.

"Yes, she has but it's to be expected. It's eight years since she left home as a young girl. Now, she's a twenty year old woman. You were nineteen when we married," Paul comforted, stroking his wife's hand.

"Since Brigitte died, her character has altered. I don't feel the same closeness to her even when she's here. I'm not sure what she's thinking anymore. Somehow there's a distance, a sort of unspoken barrier between us," Heidi dabbed the tears as she reached this conclusion.

"Certainly. Brigitte's death must have affected her greatly but I think she has changed since Alex Durnek stopped coaching her. I was passing the schoolroom yesterday and Sylvia Mietl was there. She was interested in Katya's progress. We talked for some time. She said most teenagers go through what she termed 'an awkward phase'. She said they need to establish their independence. Afterwards, they are as pleasant as they were before," said Paul, stroking his eight hour old whiskers with the inside of his right index finger, unsure if he accepted this prognosis.

"Sylvia's a knowledgeable woman and she's probably right.... But I had hoped that Katya would run in this year's Olympics and then come home for good, live in the valley, find a husband and have children......"

Heidi turned, her face streaming with tears. Paul held her to his chest, his shirt absorbing the tears.

"It's this coach, Dieter Muller, that concerns me," he whispered to the air as he stroked Heidi's hair, cradled against his breast.

Chapter 10

KATYA was now established as the D.D.R.'s fastest women's steeplechaser. Her training regime was set to increase her red blood cell count.

"Red blood cells carry the oxygen that the muscles of endurance athletes require," Dieter explained to Katya as he injected 'vitamins' into her body. "The more vitamins you take, the less fatigue and therefore the more training you can endure. The training stimulates the production of more red cells," he said, replacing the syringe in the drawer of his desk.

Katya nodded, "I think I could try four sessions a day, that is, if you want me to," she offered.

"Let's see what your blood tests show. I will need another urine sample tomorrow evening," he said.

In 1986, Katya won her first international championship. The European gold medal hung between her breasts as she watched the D.D.R. flag raised and its anthem played. When she returned to the Institute, she was given her own apartment on the campus.

In the first heat of the women's steeplechase, at the World Championships in Rome, Katya was to race Shannon Whelan of the U.S.A. for the first time. All her other major opponents were European and she had beaten them the previous year. Seventy-two hours before the race, Dieter Muller received a call from an official of the D.D.R. Sports Medical Service.

"Schmidt's not clean."

Dieter replaced the receiver on its cradle. The Direktor at the Institute would be critical when he returned. He would need to have a good explanation but, for now, he needed to deal with Katya. Her latest urine sample still showed traces of illegal substances. It was taken three days before so it was possible that she was clean now. He would arrange a further sample and send it for analysis. If he received the result by Wednesday evening and she was clean, she could race in the first heat on Thursday morning. Dieter obtained the sample and sent it for analysis. He waited and, on Wednesday evening, went to see the team manager. He explained his predicament.

"If you only sent the sample on Monday evening, it is not likely that they will receive it before tomorrow. We cannot risk a positive drug test in the competition. I will withdraw Schmidt tomorrow morning. She has food poisoning. You should get something for her from our medical team," was the clipped analysis of the team manager.

Dieter gave Katya a pink pill. "You need to take this now, before you sleep," he said.

"But I thought I didn't need vitamins within ten days of a race. I haven't been taking them," Katya responded, looking at the pill nestling in the palm of her right hand.

"That's fine but you do need to take this pill now," Dieter insisted, watching as Katya obeyed his instructions.

"Good, good, now sleep well. It's an important race tomorrow," Dieter said, closing the door behind him as he left Katya's room.

Katya woke in the night with stomach cramps. She reached the bathroom in time to vomit in the handbasin. Her room-mate awoke and spent much of the next four hours till dawn, caring for her stricken team-mate. A team doctor arrived and sedated Katya. She slept until three p.m., awaking five hours after Shannon Whelan's victory in the first heat.

At the schoolhouse, Sylvia Mietl depressed the on/off button on the television. A blank, grey screen replaced the smiling face of Shannon Whelan.

"I think Katya would have run faster," said Heidi.

"Yes, but the American girl won quite comfortably," counselled Paul.

"Well, our Katya's the best and that's that," declared the butcher, Herr Mandli, to almost universal murmurs of approval from the thirty-strong audience.

"It's a pity Katya caught food poisoning," said Heidi. "I've never known her suffer from it before. She can drink the sweetest goat's milk without effect," she continued in defence of her daughter's constitution.

"It's quite common when people travel," Sylvia said. "The organisms on food are different. The stomach needs to adjust," she finished.

Heidi nodded her acceptance of the schoolteacher's judgement.

Katya again stayed at the Institute during the summer break. She was relieved that Dieter had accepted her failure to run in Rome with such equanimity. On their return from Italy, he had taken her to a restaurant in the town for dinner. Her initial nervousness was dissipated by a glass of hock. She was flattered by his laughter at her attempted jokes. That night, she felt a peculiar new contentment as she drifted from consciousness.

★ ★ ★ ★ ★

Throughout September, Katya trained enthusiastically. Dieter often complimented her on her efforts.

"If all my athletes had your commitment, then maybe they

too would be potential Olympic champions," his words caressed her ego and tickled her heart.

"Could you come for dinner on Friday?" she asked, emboldened by his praise.

"Sure. What time and where?"

Dieter's voice stroked her eardrums. She had been planning to ask him for three weeks but the courage to face a possible rejection eluded her. Now she had taken the risk and he had accepted.

"I will cook so please come to my apartment for seven thirty," Katya replied.

Katya visited the canteen kitchen the next day. The senior cook was particularly helpful once she had explained her difficulty.

"So, you need to cook a meal for Herr Muller and yourself but you do not have the necessary experience. If you wish, I will cook for you. Then you must only take the meal from the oven and serve. Is this satisfactory to you?" he beamed, intoxicated by his own kindness.

"Would you....? Would you....? Thank you.... Thank you so much. I will pay for the ingredients, for your time," Katya gushed appreciatively.

"On Friday afternoon, at three, I will prepare a venison stew with onions, carrots and turnips. I will make my special thick stock to blend these tastes. Fifteen minutes before you take it from the oven, you must mix in the bowl of blackcurrants I will have prepared for you. Also, I will leave four pieces of cured ham, paper thin and two pears. Cut the peel from the pears and slice the fruit onto the ham. This is a good entrée. Do you need a dessert?"

"I'm fine for dessert. Dieter likes ice cream so I will get some," Katya replied.

"There are still strawberries if you need some with the ice cream," the cook offered.

"Thank you, yes please," Katya responded, kissing the rotund cook on his balding pate.

Dieter clapped his stomach with his hands, "That was marvellous, Katya. The wine, the deer was so tender, the starter and ice cream with strawberries. How did you find the time?"

Katya's face glowed from his compliment. She could feel the heat rise on her cheeks. She tried to slow the effect by patting them with her fingertips.

"It wasn't only me," she confessed. "The cook from the canteen did most of the meal for me."

"Well, whatever, it was splendid," said Dieter rising. "I must go now but that was excellent."

They kissed each other on the cheeks as Dieter left. "Thank you for the chocolates," said Katya as she held the door open for him.

Chapter 11

OCTOBER, 1987

"DIETER, we need to discuss Katya Schmidt's training results," said the Direktor, opening a blue folder on his desk.

"Her blood tests are good for this time of year, Herr Direktor," replied Dieter, reading from his own folder.

"Her training times, how are her training times?" the Direktor pressed.

"She continues to show progress. She is faster than October last year, Herr Direktor," responded Dieter.

"You have the gold standard we have set for her event in Seoul?" he asked.

"Yes, Herr Direktor."

"And . . . ."

"Oh, Herr Direktor . . . you mean . . . sorry . . . I'm pleased to say she is currently two seconds inside the gold standard time."

"And the world record?"

"It's the same time as the gold standard Herr Direktor."

"Good, good but we must make sure that she wins in a record time for the glory of the Deutsche Democratic Republic."

"Yes, Herr Direktor."

"So . . . Dieter we have been conducting studies. Women's bodies produce more red blood cells when they are pregnant. This is a useful attribute for an endurance athlete and the steeplechase is an endurance event?"

"Yes, Herr Direktor."

"I want to try a new experiment. I want Katya Schmidt to start a pregnancy in December this year."

Dieter waited for the Direktor to continue, then realised that he had finished speaking and was awaiting his response.

"But, Herr Direktor, she will be eight months pregnant when she competes in the Seoul Olympics. I don't think she could jump the hurdles."

"She won't be pregnant then. Our work has shown that the benefit of increased red blood cells lasts for many months after the end of a pregnancy."

"How are we to do this Herr Direktor?"

"We will terminate the pregnancy eight weeks before her final. Our tests have shown that, with her pills, she should be able to continue training with just two days' interruption for the abortion."

"Herr Direktor, Katya's already running fast enough to win and, hopefully, in world record time."

"Hopefully is not good enough. I need to know that she will win in world record time and, to do this, we should follow the scientific advice we've been given."

"Maybe so but, looking at the practicalities, she needs someone to make her pregnant and she doesn't even have a boyfriend," Dieter argued.

"You are the coach. How it is done is up to you," the Direktor was tiring of the procrastination.

"I'm fond of her. I don't want her to be hurt..." Dieter spoke sharply.

"Good, if you are fond of her, that should make it easier for you...You won't have to drug her and rape her," concluded the Direktor, writing in the file in front of him.

Dieter sat watching. He admonished himself for his

questioning. Experience had shown him that obedience to those in authority was the surest path to promotion.

The Direktor finished writing and closed the file.

"Herr Muller, do you have a problem with my instructions?" the Director demanded.

"No, no, Herr Direktor," Dieter replied, quickly.

"You do not want to suffer the same fate as Herr Durnek. He found it too difficult to put the interests of the State before his feelings for the athletes."

"Herr Direktor, I will carry out the task you have set me."

"Dieter, do you understand why this Institute exists, it's importance to the success of our State?"

"We exist to bring sporting glory to the D.D.R., to show through sport that Communism is superior to capitalism," Dieter proudly parroted what he had been taught.

"Yes, yes, this is partly true but there is more kudos to be gained in beating the other Communist countries than beating the west. Our leaders stand taller at Warsaw Pact conferences because of our sporting superiority. The zenith would be to win more Olympic gold medals than the Soviets. This is our mission. We achieved this in the Winter Olympics in Sarajevo in 1984 for the first time. The Soviets were fearful that we might beat them in the Summer Games in Los Angeles. They boycotted them and instructed the D.D.R. to show solidarity. They have taken a deep interest in our training programmes since. This is why we must push the science harder and harder. Athletes are expendable. Do you understand?"

"Yes, Herr Direktor. I understand," replied Dieter.

"Good, good. I will see if I can get you a bigger apartment. I will note your positive attitude in my next report."

"Thank you, Herr Direktor."

Chapter 12

DIETER plotted his seduction of Katya. He noted that the 16th of October was her twenty-fourth birthday. At the end of the next training session, he approached her.

"Katya, it's your birthday next Saturday," he said, nonchalantly taking hold of her right hand. "I still haven't repaid you for that wonderful meal two weeks ago," he continued, gently squeezing her fingers. "Please allow me to take you to the theatre in Dresden in honour of your anniversary?" he asked.

"Yes... yes... that would be great," Katya exclaimed.

"We could go to a restaurant after the show if you like," Dieter suggested.

"I would like that. Yes please," Katya responded excitedly.

"Fine, I will arrange for a car to take us. I will pick you up at your apartment at three p.m."

Katya had bees inside her head, a drummer in her chest and dizziness in her thighs as she walked to her apartment. "Wow," pinballed through her body.

She sat at the table looking out of the window across the campus, contemplating the evening in Dresden with Dieter. She hadn't anticipated her birthday with such excitement since she was twelve. That was the last birthday she had celebrated at home with her friends. Monika, Sasha, Helga and Nadia had slept over; she smiled fondly at the memory. Now, twelve years later, in two days, she would go to Dresden with Dieter and...... her libidinous thoughts tingled the tips of her breasts. Katya plotted the seduction of her coach.

Dieter rang the doorbell to Katya's apartment at five minutes to three on Friday afternoon.

"Hi," Katya answered the door, kissing both of Dieter's cheeks with her lips.

"You look stunning," Dieter stammered, thrilled by the warmth of the welcome.

"Thank you. I'm pleased you approve," Katya replied, twirling three hundred and sixty degrees. The red gypsy skirt flowed from her hips as she span. Her white bodice top was off her shoulders. Her perfume, released by the twirl, smote Dieter's olfactory nerve ends.

Katya picked up her red handbag and a red shawl. "I'm ready," she said, taking Dieter's arm and pulling the door closed. Her red, stiletto-heeled shoes clacked on the concrete steps.

The driver held the rear kerbside door of the taxi open and Katya climbed in. Dieter had walked around to the offside door, his senses still numbed by the effect Katya was creating on them.

As they chatted and laughed during the forty-five minute drive to the city, they each found cause to touch the other's knee.

"It's not quite four o'clock," said Dieter as their car drew into the kerbside in Theatreplatz, outside the Opera House. "Shall we walk along the river? There is a small café . . . ."

Dieter paused, aware that Katya had got out of the car. He instructed the driver to return to the Institute and then walked around the car to stand beside her. "It's magnificent isn't it?" he said, following her eyes up the facade of the Opera House. "Later, you will see the inside which is even more splendid."

Katya's mouth formed a perfect o. Dieter chuckled with pleasure at the effect.

"Yes," he answered her unasked question. "We have tickets for the Opera here tonight, at seven."

Katya squealed, grasping Dieter's head and kissing him fiercely on the cheek.

"Would you like to go for a coffee and perhaps a slice of torte? I know a . . . . . . "

"Yes, please," Katya interrupted, clasping Dieter's right hand with her left.

They walked beside the river, following its flow but at a slower pace.

"I grew up beside a river," Katya mused as golden, autumn leaves swept by in the current, chased by russets and reds. "Well, not really a river, more a stream in the valley and just a rill where it passes our chalet."

"Tell me more. I'd like to know more of your childhood," Dieter pressed, his hand squeezing Katya's and his voice pitched for acquiescence.

Thirty minutes later, as they pushed open the door of the café, Dieter knew the names of Katya's friends, her school-teacher, her parents and her favourite goats. He could picture in his mind, the bedroom she slept in, the table she ate at.

"Yummee . . . ," Katya exclaimed as she studied the array of cakes in front of her.

Choices made, Katya sat at a table by the window sipping her coffee between forkfuls of chocolate ganache.

"Dieter, you should tell me more of your history, where you grew up, how you became a coach. Do you have brothers or sisters?"

"Mmm, let me see . . . . I was born on May the 5th. The year was 1951. My parents had three earlier children and none after so I was the youngest of four. All three of my siblings were girls. I attended school in Liepzig and then the College for Physical Culture for four years. There, I qualified as a coach and was fortunate to receive a post at the Institute. Does this solve your curiosity?"

Katya nodded an agreement which belied her thoughts. She would have liked to have known the names of his sisters, their ages, what they were doing now, did Dieter still contact them and much, much more of his history but she sensed his reticence so did not press. Katya sipped the last of her coffee.

They walked back along the river, its passengers, leaves, sticks and waterfowl now rushing towards them. They passed under the railway bridge as a train clanked by above their heads. Katya picked up a small, flat stone from the ground by her feet and sent it skimming across the surface of the water, one . . . . two . . . . . . three . . . . four . . . five . . . six.

She picked up another flat stone. Her outstretched arm offered the toy to Dieter.

"Your turn now. More than six to win."

Dieter took the stone and dropped it into the water. "I don't play this game," he said as the ripples from his stone lapped the water's edge. They continued their stroll in silence. Katya's heart jumped faster as she tried to adjust to Dieter's new mood. Perhaps he thinks me too frivolous she considered, doubt whipping her self-esteem.

At six thirty, they stood outside the Opera House.

"Would you like a glass of wine before the performance?" Dieter asked with a broad smile which released the tension from Katya's body.

"Yes please," she replied as Dieter escorted her into the foyer. "Wow," Katya exclaimed, turning on her heel to absorb the majesty of the interior.

"They finished the restoration two years ago," said Dieter, pleased with Katya's reaction.

Dieter held the inside of Katya's right forearm gently between the fingers of his left hand as he led her to the bar. The sweet, cool wine caressed her inside as the golden décor tingled the surface of her skin. The hubbub of sound caused Dieter to place his lips close to her right ear. Katya swept her hair behind the ear to attend. The vibrations of the air between his moving lips and her ear tickled the fuzz on her lobe in a fashion that tightened the skin on her left breast exquisitely. The novel sensations weakened the resolve of her legs. Dieter caught her around the waist as she swooned. The dizziness passed in a few seconds.

"Are you sick?" he asked.

"No.... No... I think it's delirium caused by happiness," Katya smiled ecstatically.

"Oh," Dieter responded, perplexed.

"I'm fine, really, I'm fine," Katya assured.

"Let's go to our seats then. Perhaps you will feel better if you are seated," Dieter explained, still unconvinced of Katya's well-being, fearful that his seduction might be thwarted by her illness.

By the end of the performance, Katya appeared to be fully recovered. Ebullience flowed from her excited chatter.

"That was terrific, absolutely fantastic, momentous, mystical, magical, mem......," the superlatives burst from her mouth, enveloping Dieter in a blanket of new hope.

"The restaurant is ten minutes walk or would you prefer a taxi? They're very hard to find this late," he said rhetorically, leading Katya by the hand towards the Augustus Bridge.

As they crossed the bridge over the Elbe, leaving the Altstadt, Katya stopped to watch the moonlit water swirl by below.

"Thank you, thank you, this is the best birthday ever," she squeezed Dieter's fingers so tightly, he had to shake the circulation back into them when she loosened her grip.

69

"There's more. I think you will enjoy the restaurant and, if you wish, we could go dancing afterwards. I know of a discothèque in a hotel close by," Dieter probed.

"Yes, yes. I'd love to dance," Katya trilled.

"Here's the restaurant," Dieter smiled, pushing open the green, painted, wooden door. A formally dressed maitre d' greeted them, head cocked in inquisition, pen poised above the open page of his reservations ledger.

"Muller, my table for two," Dieter requested.

"Ah yes, Herr Muller," the maitre d' ticked the entry with his pen. "Welcome. This way please," he said, plucking two leather-bound menus from the shelf in his lectern.

Most of the candlelit tables were occupied as they passed. The maitre d' stopped beside an empty table for two, set in an alcove.

"Voila, Herr Muller," he nodded to Dieter and pulled a chair away from the table. "Mademoiselle," he said, bowing to Katya.

Four thousand calories and a bottle of the D.D.R's finest champagne later, Dieter left a small pile of ostmarks on the saucer as he took the bill and folded it into his wallet.

"Do you still wish to dance?" Dieter asked Katya, glancing at the face of his wristwatch. "It would be too late to get a taxi back to the Institute if we go to a club now," he continued.

"I would love to dance. Today has been so memorable, I don't want it to end," she cooed, placing her right forearm on Dieter's proffered left arm as they walked out of the now near empty restaurant.

"We can stay at the hotel which has the club. I'm sure we can get a couple of rooms," he said confidently.

"O K... let's go," Katya hiccupped, the consumption of three quarters of a bottle of sparkling wine taking effect on her diaphragm.

Dieter had little talent in dancing so, after an hour, they took the elevator from the basement club to the foyer of the hotel.

"You wait here," Dieter advised Katya as they exited the lift. Dieter returned two minutes later, shaking his head, "They only have one room available," he said, feigning regret.

"That's not a problem; let's go," Katya replied with no hint of concern. The lift took them to the fifth floor. The room had one queen-sized bed and a separate bathroom.

"Do you mind if I go first?" pleaded Katya, entering the bathroom.

Dieter smiled and sat on the corner of the bed. He undid the laces on his shoes, slipping his heels and then his toes from them. He pulled on the end of his right sock which slid from his foot and then did the same with his left foot. He pulled his shirt, damp from the exertions of his dancing, over his head and stood. He fiddled with the buckle on his belt, unsure as to the appropriate timing for the removal of his trousers. Katya came out of the bathroom and stood before him in all her natural beauty.

Dieter finished unbuckling, unzipped and let his trousers fall about his ankles. Katya hooked her thumbs inside the elasticated waistband of his under shorts and thrust them to his knees. She took hold of his shoulders and pulled him down onto the bed grasping his now rampant member.

Dieter's skill at lovemaking was similar to his talent at dancing. He fumbled for his condom and then dropped it. Then, when fully recovered and encased, he climbed on top of Katya. He squashed her breasts in his hands, humped for four minutes until his seed shot and then he rolled off. He put the used condom on the bedside table next to his watch and slept. Katya brought herself to a climax as he snored.

"Well, I suppose he can't be an expert at everything," she

thought, mentally comparing him to the boys at the Institute and their prowess. Dieter must be just about the worst lover she had ever had. She knew she had a very high sex drive. Many of the girls at the Institute she had talked to seemed to have heightened sexual needs. The consensus was that the pink and blue vitamin pills somehow dramatically increased libido.

Katya was asleep when Dieter woke. He looked at her sleeping form. In two months, he would need to impregnate her. He calculated that he would need to continue the seduction and dispense with the protective after her December period. Dieter noticed his debris on the bedside table. Semen had leaked from the protective and was pooled around the face of his wristwatch. He fetched tissue from the bathroom to clear up his mess.

The sexual relationship between Katya and Dieter bumped along over the following eight weeks with little improvement in his technique. Katya had made no complaint, fearful she might bruise Dieter's ego. Her biological cycle now complete, Katya, in her optimism, decided that their next conjunction would be more satisfying. Dieter knocked on the door of Katya's apartment. "Tonight will be the night," he exhorted himself. His right hand clutched a bottle of D.D.R. champagne. A box of white and dark chocolate truffles, grasped in his left hand, almost dislodged as his knuckles beat upon the door.

Katya opened the door to her present-laden lover.

"Dieter, is this a special occasion?" Katya exclaimed, noticing his gifts.

"No, no.... well yes....," Dieter stammered, his face pinking guiltily as he entered her apartment.

Katya kissed the blushing cheeks. Dieter stood, hands occupied as Katya's fingers locked behind his neck and drew his mouth to her lips. The effect was electric as the tip of her tongue probed the inside of his cheek. All the nerve endings in his body were shocked by the sensation. His eyelids fluttered and closed to capture the intensity of the moment. Katya released him, withdrawing her tongue.

"I'll get some glasses," she said as her fingers slipped from his neck.

Twenty minutes later, they lay side by side on the sheepskin rug, clothes strewn about the floor. Most of the bottle of sparkling wine fizzed inside them. Dieter rolled on top of Katya but Katya used his momentum to continue his roll and at the end of the tumble she was on top. She sat astride Dieter, her pudendum squashed against his hairy stomach.

"Now, Herr Coach," she said with mock sternness, "You must be the student and I will be the teacher." Katya raised her hips and thrust her right hand between her legs balancing with her left hand on Dieter's chest. She grasped his member and squeezed, pulling its tip towards her vagina. She sat back, forcing his manhood deep inside her. Katya gyrated her hips, grinding their pubic bones together. She used the power in her thigh muscles to ride, her fingers spread on Dieter's chest. She sensed a tensing in Dieter's stomach. Katya sat motionless until the tension subsided. She controlled the pace of their lovemaking. This was the most satisfying sex she had ever had. She rode on until she arrived. Her back arched, her head arched, the muscles in her legs tightened, her whole body was in spasm. The muscles in her vagina tightened around Dieter's manhood.

Katya lay on Dieter's chest, listening to the beat of their racing pulses subside. Ten minutes later, she went to the bathroom to shower off the perspiration from her ride. Dieter lay on the rug, smiling to himself. The transition was so much easier than he had imagined. He'd expected some difficulty, some resistance to the lack of a protective. He'd planned to say that he'd forgotten and hoped that she didn't keep her own supply. Katya was due to leave for the Christmas break in seven days so he would try to service her each day until then.

Chapter 13

PAUL and Heidi noticed the sparkle in Katya's demeanour when she returned. During the two weeks of her visit, Dieter's name was constant. Whether in an athletics or social context, Katya continually referenced him.

After Katya had returned to the Institute, Heidi sat at the meal table, her hands clasped around a mug of warm, honeyed goat's milk.

"She seems very happy. I think she's gone back early to be with this man, Dieter," she said, thoughtfully seeking Paul's opinion.

"Yes, I think you are right.... but I'm worried about such a relationship," he murmured, unsure of his right to opine on such a subject.

"Huh... don't be so old fashioned, Paul. I know he is twelve years older but, if they love each other...."

"It's not the age difference. It's the fact that he is her coach. There is no room for romance in that relationship. The focus must always be on performance.... Anyway, it's old fashioned to accept big age gaps between husband and wife. That's the way of our forefathers," Paul stated, responding to Heidi's barb.

"Perhaps if you met him?" Heidi conciliated.

"Yes, maybe... but I don't agree with all these vitamin pills he gives her. Why can't she just eat properly?" Paul responded, refusing to be placated.

"Well, the Olympics are in less than eight months.

Hopefully she'll win her gold then settle down and we will have grandchildren. No more pills," Heidi said brightly.

The week that Katya returned to the Institute was the regular time for her period. Dieter knew this from his records. Katya also knew but she had none of her usual premenstrual symptoms. However, she was still keen to have more sex with Dieter and he obliged.

Three weeks after her return, Katya's biological clock was still showing the wrong time. Dieter suggested she take a pregnancy test. This returned a positive result.

Katya was aghast. Over the past few weeks, she had considered that she might be pregnant but without really contemplating the consequences. Now she was and her life's ambition to become an Olympic champion was threatened. She had risked all for a few moments of pleasure. She knew she preferred the absence of a protective. Psychologically, physiologically, it was more satisfying. What would her parents say? What would the villagers think? The cascade of questions, the crescendo of scenarios clashed inside her head.

Dieter arrived, having been informed by the Institute's Senior Medical Officer. Katya talked to him through the door. "Leave me alone," she pleaded. "I need time ... time to think."

Dieter resisted his inclination to dominate. "When you're ready, I will be at my apartment," he said as he walked from her doorway.

Katya let her mind run riot. She sat in her armchair and waited as the mayhem inside her head ricocheted relentlessly. Some hours after, the stars appeared in the sky. She rose from her seat, closed the curtains and went to her bed. She knew then that she would have the pregnancy terminated.

When Katya awoke the next afternoon, she visited Dieter, certain that he would approve of her decision. Katya left five minutes later and returned to her own apartment. She was stunned by Dieter's reaction. He seemed unconcerned by the prospect of her not running in the Olympics.

"There's always Barcelona. You'll only be twenty-eight, still in your athletic prime," he'd lectured angrily.

"What about us? The foetus growing inside of you?" he demanded.

This was one scenario Katya had not considered. She'd never imagined her pregnancy as a baby. She thought of it as an injury, a malady that needed to be cured.

Dieter was right. He was always right. They were going to have a baby. She was going to be a mother. These thoughts washed warmth throughout her body. Her parents would have a grandchild. If Dieter would agree, they could marry tomorrow. People would talk when the baby came so quickly but at least it wouldn't be a bastard. Her ambition to be an Olympic Champion could wait four years until Barcelona. Her final conscious thoughts that evening were that married women with children had won Olympic gold medals in the past.

Dieter was pleased with Katya's new decision. He agreed that marriage was a good idea and that it should happen before the baby was born. Katya accepted his wisdom. He asked her to continue training as her example helped motivate the other athletes in the squad. Surprisingly, Katya's times continued to improve. Each time Katya mentioned marriage, Dieter agreed that it should happen soon but not quite yet. By June, the bump on Katya's tummy was showing even against the loosest training top. Katya was called to the clinic for her regular fortnightly injection. That evening, as she ate dinner with Dieter, she doubled over with abdominal cramps. Dieter took her back to the clinic where she spent the night sedated after the removal of her foetus.

Katya returned to her apartment the next day. Two days later she was back on the training track.

"It was necessary, Katya. Your life was in danger. They had to remove the foetus. It's gone."

"My baby is dead!" cried Katya. "It was twenty-eight weeks old."

"You would have died. If you still want the gold medal, you'll have to move on," Dieter's harsh words stung as they landed on Katya's eardrums. She wanted to shriek, to pound the insensitivity out of Dieter's body with her fists. Instead, she walked away sobbing.

Chapter 14

WEEKS passed. Katya was now running faster than ever before. The aching eased as the guilty excitement of the Seoul Olympics took hold. Her parents knew nothing of her pregnancy and she determined not to tell them. Many letters had arrived from the village wishing her success in Korea. She had been officially selected to represent the D.D.R. in the women's three thousand metres steeplechase. Several other athletes at the Institute had also been chosen to compete for the D.D.R.

The atmosphere was expectant. Conversations were almost exclusively Olympics related. Uniforms arrived to travel in and to attend the Opening Ceremony. Tracksuits and running kit together with team kitbags were delivered, each emblazoned with the Stechzirkel and hammer symbol now internationally synonymous with world-beating athletic prowess. As she caressed the logo with the tips of the middle two fingers of her right hand, Katya's memory was stimulated. Sylvia Mietl had taught them the meaning of this logo. The dividers represented the engineers and the hammer, the workers. Together they would build a stronger nation. From her limited international experiences, Katya knew the respect, even fear, that this logo engendered in competitors from other countries.

The team flew from East Berlin's Tegel airport on the 12th September, 1988 to Seoul in South Korea. Only athletes, coaches, physiotherapists, team doctors and Stasi secret police, accredited as team officials, boarded the plane. On arrival in Seoul, the team was hustled through the welcoming protocols at the airport on to buses to the Olympic village. In the village, they had their own quarters. At mealtimes, they were encouraged to sit together, escorted by their Stasi minders. Fraternisation with members of other teams was discouraged. Katya, who had been taken off pills four weeks before, obeyed the rules and focussed on the training programme that Dieter set. He was pleased with her progress through the heats, nervous after her easy victory in the semi-final and ecstatic after she won the final in a new world record time, beating the American, Shannon Whelan, into second place by over fifty metres. Her muscles, with an ample supply of oxygen, had transmitted none of the searing pain felt by her fellow competitors as they trailed behind her.

Katya stood inside her dreams atop the centre step of the medal podium in the Olympic stadium. The gold medal hung between her breasts. The D.D.R. national anthem played as the black, red and yellow tricolour with the Stechzirkel logo in the centre of the red band was raised above all others.

In the schoolhouse in the village, Heidi and Paul wept as they watched their daughter on the television. Tears trickled down the lines in Sylvia Mietl's weathered face.

"You always had faith, Paul. You told me she could be an Olympic champion," the old teacher patted Paul's shoulder as she spoke.

"She's the best we've ever produced," declared Herr Mandli, the butcher, adopting Katya's success as a product of the village.

Back in the Olympic village, Katya was feted by her fellow team members. Journalists and television broadcasters clamoured for interviews. Dieter crushed her in the fiercest embrace she could remember.

"We must stay together now Katya," he said, releasing his grip.

"Yes Dieter... yes we must ....," she replied, bewildered and elated.

"Let's get a coffee and some cake," he offered, taking her hand and drawing her through the melee at the media centre.

"Was your urine sample easy?" he asked as they walked towards the dining hall.

"No problem. What with the excitement of winning, I was through in five minutes," Katya laughed.

Chocolate cake surrounded Katya's lips as she gorged on her third slice. She dropped half of the wedge onto her plate, her eyes bulging from their sockets.

"Beaten?" Dieter enquired, "Well, that's the first time you've been beaten at these Olympics," he chortled, pleased with his own humour. Katya smiled, pleased that Dieter was so happy.

"You will be a major celebrity when we return home. Sporting excellence is highly regarded by our leaders. A new world record at the Olympics is rare. They may even name a street in your honour."

Katya smiled at Dieter's enthusiasm. He continued, "Some of the honour will attach to me as your coach but you can expect most of the rewards, a bigger, more stylish apartment, your own car, access to the special stores, dinners with members of the Central Committee – men of real power and authority." Dieter glowed in the glory he anticipated for them.

After the coffee and cake, they returned to the room Dieter shared with another coach. The room was unoccupied. Katya had sex with Dieter for the first time in four months.

Katya's celebrity status, when they returned to the D.D.R., was everything Dieter had forecast. Her diary was controlled by Dieter. He knew which invitations had to be accepted and those that could be replied to with an apology. Katya insisted on visiting her parents for Christmas. She had not been back to their village since her victory in Seoul.

Paul and Heidi shared their daughter's homecoming with the villagers. Five hours after the reception began, Katya drove them home in her new car. She slept in her own bed, Adie clasped to her breast. It was ten a.m. before she awoke the next morning. Katya walked into her mother's kitchen in her pyjamas.

"You slept well?" Heidi enquired, kissing her daughter's left cheek.

"Yessss...," Katya yawned, stretching her arms over and behind her head.

"I'll get you some breakfast. I have a fine ham that Herr Mandli has given me for you. It's the best I have ever tasted. Sit down and I will bring it to you," Heidi instructed.

Katya took a plate from the dresser shelf and a knife and fork from the drawer. Heidi placed a half loaf of fresh, crusted bread on a wooden board on the table with a bread saw next to Katya's plate as Katya returned with a five kilo ham dangling from her right hand and a jug of milk in her left.

"Would you like a piece of goat's cheese with your ham?" Heidi asked.

"Yes please," Katya replied, cutting a slice from the ham with the bread saw. "Mmm....," she murmured, picking up some crumbled fragments. "It's delicious," she said as Heidi put an empty mug and the dish of cheese on the table.

After all the banquets of the past three months, Katya's tummy was grateful for the plain country fare.

"I'll just get dressed. Then we can go for a walk by the stream if you like," Katya suggested as she cleared the table.

"Yes, I would like that," Heidi replied, taking the crockery and cutlery to dunk under the suds in her blue, plastic, washing-up bowl.

Ten days after she arrived, Katya waved from her car window to her parents as she drove down the track away from her parents' chalet. She had enjoyed the tranquillity, the company of Paul and Heidi, the simple, fresh food. However, the past few days had also been stressful. It was clear from their conversations that her mother wanted her to quit athletics, return to the village, marry and produce grandchildren. Her father, whilst not so outspoken on the need for her to 'settle down', was obviously unhappy about her relationship with Dieter.

Katya was pleased she was leaving. Her thoughts turned to her destination. She was beginning to yearn for the hurly-burly of her life in the city. She missed Dieter. He had moved into her new apartment in Dresden. They both had cars so could easily commute to the training track. She was reconciled to his foibles, his infrequent flashes of petulance, more frequent attacks of flatulence and his petty selfishness. Katya believed the latter was a result of him growing up with three older sisters to spoil him.

After two hours driving, Katya parked in her allotted bay beside her apartment block. She opened her front door and called, "Hi, I'm back." The quiet response told her Dieter was out. She picked up the note he had left beside the telephone.

Katya,

I am celebrating with some friends from the Institute this evening. Don't wait up for me as I will probably stay overnight. See you at the track tomorrow.

Yours, Dieter X

Chapter 15

THE 1989 athletics season was a confusion of receptions, training, celebrity appearances and photo sessions. At the end of the season, Katya ran in the World Cup final in Barcelona. Despite the distractions, she was able to win. Her major challengers from Seoul were absent and her winning time was fifteen seconds slower than her Olympic final. Dieter was delighted. He knew that Katya had missed a substantial amount of training and was some way from peak fitness.

Katya invited Heidi and Paul to Dresden for Sylvester. There was ample room in her apartment. Only one of the two bedrooms was being used and Dieter had reluctantly agreed to leave for the three days they would be staying. Katya's clinching argument was that the alternative would be a trip home and she would miss the Grand Sylvester Ball. Dieter knew his ticket to the gathering of the powerful and influential depended on Katya's presence. She now also had sufficient influence to obtain tickets to the Opera House for her parents' visit.

Heidi and Paul were impressed by the scale of Katya's apartment and mesmerised by the beauty of the Opera House. Katya omitted all reference to Dieter, cutting short any attempt by her parents to introduce him as a subject in their conversations. When they left, on the train, each felt relief that Katya's relationship with her coach had definitely cooled.

Katya let the straps from her ball gown slip from her shoulders. She stepped out of the dress.

"There was a lot of talk about the future," Dieter said, unclipping his black bow tie. "Since the opening of the Berlin Wall, nothing is certain anymore. One of the Central Committee members even confided that we could be re-united with the West," he said, placing his gold cufflinks in his jewellery box.

"What does that mean?" asked Katya, sliding her panties from her hips.

"I'm not sure but 1990 will be an eventful year for us," he stated, climbing under the duvet and snuggling against Katya's warm body.

Dieter cut back on Katya's extra-curricula activities during 1990. His reputation in a now to be re-united Germany was dependent on Katya's continued success. He increased the time spent training and the intensity of the sessions. Katya felt almost constantly fatigued. The blue and pink pills were withdrawn as were the injections. Dieter assured her that the sports scientists had discovered that diet was more critical to optimum performance than vitamin supplements. Katya wrote to her father with the news that his nostrum was now the accepted scientific remedy for muscle fatigue.

Katya successfully defended her European Championship title at Split in Yugoslavia that summer. The searing pain in her thighs reminded her of the time trials she had ran for Alex Durnek. The intensity of the agony, a long-lost friend banished by the vitamin pills, had now returned.

Dieter was pleased. "I told you diet was the better solution," he said, hugging her as she dismounted the victory rostrum with a further gold medal bouncing between her breasts.

That autumn, Dieter and Katya went on holiday for two weeks. They had been offered a lakeside cabin by a member of the Central Committee. The setting was idyllic. Dieter behaved impeccably. His self-interest abated as he deferred more to Katya's likes and dislikes. Katya began to think that maybe she was in love.

The day after they returned from their vacation, Dieter was summonsed to the Direktor's office.

The Direktor's intense, grey eyes dominated his underling. Then he spoke.

"Dieter, come in, sit down," the Direktor instructed, smiling as he pointed to a chair in front of his desk.

"Dieter it's over. The D.D.R. is finished. It's just a comma in the history of Germany now."

"But ... ... in a unified Germany."

"Don't frown so. It is not your fault. I did my job and you were an obedient subordinate. We conquered the world. Our athletes became the best in the world," said the Direktor, eyes sparkling with tears as he recollected his triumph. "Our knowledge, our training systems and the data we collected make us very valuable in the international sports' market."

"What happens to us? Does that mean our employment stops? When does my employment stop?" quizzed Dieter, oblivious to his boss's fustian.

"You haven't been listening ... ... It's over, finished. You have no job in the new Germany. The centre is closed. The Stasi didn't destroy all the records. Now, as we sit here, people are piecing together the documents they shredded."

"How long can I keep the apartment?" Dieter asked.

"I don't know. It doesn't matter. I'm telling you, we did our job. If the central planners and the politicians had succeeded as we did ... ... but they didn't so we must move on. What was achieved here is the envy of the sporting world."

"What about Katya?" Dieter said, rhetorically.

"Katya ... Katya who?" demanded the Direktor.

"Katya Schmidt, the Olympic steeplechase champion," Dieter responded quietly.

"Oh, the athlete... we don't need the athletes anymore. We have the knowledge. We know the techniques, the chemistry to create new champions. That is why I called you here."

"I don't understand," Dieter said wearily.

"Just because the D.D.R. is finished doesn't mean we have to lose. I have been offered the job of Direktor of Coaching by five other nations. They are so keen to have my knowledge that they will pay up to TWENTY times my current salary. I have accepted an offer from Australia. You can come as my assistant."

"When would we start?" Dieter asked.

"Tomorrow," replied the Direktor.

Dieter walked out of the Institute for the last time. He waited outside their apartment block until he saw Katya leave. Then he went in, packed his belongings in two suitcases, scribbled a note and left it on the floor inside the front door.

Katya,

I have a new job in another country.
I will be well paid.
Do not worry about me.
Oh and anything I have left behind, you can keep.

Dieter.

Chapter 16

15th DECEMBER, 1990

THE late afternoon sun, low in the sky, shone its tired rays through the kitchen window of the Schmidt's chalet. Heidi sat in the wooden rocker, her arms resting on the side supports. She rocked gently backwards, forwards, backwards, forwards. The arched strips of wood ground the grit under them as she tick-tocked in time with the clock. Her open eyes faced the window but they saw nothing. Her mind was totally consumed with concern for her only child, Katya. Her mother's heart ached to fill the void within her.

The chalet door latch clacked, breaking her entrancement. Paul closed the door. Heidi rose from the rocking chair and embraced him. Paul felt her tremble in his arms, sensed the sharpness and intensity of her hug.

"Katya?" he said, knowing the answer.

"Yes. It's three months since we had a letter," said Heidi, releasing her spouse from her embrace.

"She hasn't written for more than three months in the past. It's not so unusual," said Paul, trying to ease his wife's anxiety.

"Paul, this is different. I just know that something is not right. I've never been comfortable with Dieter. He's stopping her from contacting us. He's taken our daughter from us," Heidi replied, pacing to and fro.

"Ah... Dieter, Herr Muller," Paul spat out the words as

if removing a bad taste from his mouth. "You may be right.... .... But if he has, what can we do? Katya's twenty-six now."

"Twenty-seven," Heidi corrected.

"Twenty-seven," Paul confirmed. "She has her own life to lead in the city. We can't bring her back here. If she wants to be with Muller, then I don't see what we can do. We could drive her away forever if we interfere," Paul counselled.

"She's our flesh. She's of our blood. We have to help her," Heidi pleaded.

"Alright, alright," Paul relented. "If we haven't had any contact over Christmas and Sylvester, we will go to Dresden, to her apartment....," he offered. "But she will probably walk through the door in the next week or so," Paul surmised optimistically.

"She's never not been with us for the New Year," Heidi responded.

For the next seventeen days, Heidi waited expectantly. She wished, she prayed, she talked to the sun, she implored the full moon, she begged the mountains but the clack of the door was never Katya. She placed Katya's Christmas presents on her bed alongside her unopened birthday gifts.

On the 2nd of January, Paul and Heidi boarded the train for Dresden in nervously optimistic anticipation.

"I hope she's not angry that we've come to see her," Paul fretted.

"Why would she be? We have her presents. It is us that have reason to be cross. She hasn't answered our letters. She hasn't come to see us even though she has a car. I've tried to telephone her from the post office every week for the past month," Heidi stoutly defended her right to visit.

At the Hauptbahnhof in Dresden, they left the train. Heidi had Katya's address in Antonsplatz.

"Do you remember the direction?" she asked Paul.

"I have a city map Katya gave me last year when we visited," Paul replied, pulling the map from inside his jacket pocket.

"We are here," he said, indicating the main train station. Pointing to an X Katya had drawn by Antonsplatz, he continued,

"We need to get here, Antonsplatz. If we leave this square at the corner over there," he pointed diagonally left, "We will then cross Wienerstrasse into Reitbahnstrasse. At the end of that street, we cross Budapesterstrasse into Marienstrasse. Antonsplatz should be a few hundred metres on the right," Paul concluded confidently.

Five minutes later, they stood apprehensively at the entrance to Katya's apartment. Paul scanned the names beside each apartment bell number. No Schmidt. He read again taking extra care. There was no K. Schmidt. Also, all the name cards appeared to be new.

"What number in Antonsplatz?" he asked.

"Fifteen," Heidi replied, checking her note.

"This is number fifteen," Paul confirmed, reading the number from the pillar beside the door.

"It was apartment seven, I remember," Heidi said.

"The bells only have names, no numbers," Paul replied. "Are we sure this is Antonsplatz?" he queried.

"Don't you remember? This is the right building," Heidi affirmed.

"Yes, I do but I'll just check before I disturb anyone," he said, walking twenty metres to the corner to confirm the place name.

"Yes," he called as he stood beneath the plaque on the wall.

Heidi counted the bell buttons and pushed the seventh from the top. Paul returned.

"I've rung the seventh bell," Heidi told him.

They waited for a response. Heidi pressed the button again.

"You won't find anyone there at this time," said an old lady walking by.

"Why?" asked Heidi. "Our daughter lives here."

"Is she married to one of the bankers then?" the old lady cackled and walked on.

Heidi's disquiet was now making way for fear. She stopped the next passer-by.

"Do you know anyone who lives here?" she asked.

"No, sorry. I'm from Frankfurt," he explained.

Paul rang the top bell. Fifteen seconds later, he heard a click. He pulled on the front door which opened. Relief washed fear from their hearts as they walked up the stairs to Katya's apartment on the first floor. Paul rapped his knuckles on the black door. Silence echoed back each time he smote the door with increasing force.

"Katya, Katya," Heidi called to the empty air.

Ten minutes of quiet persuaded them that no one was at home. Paul's reddened knuckles beat upon the other three apartment doors on the first floor.

"I'll put a note under her door," Heidi said, scribbling on her small shopping list pad. "Then she'll know we are here."

On the ground floor, Paul knocked on the doors of the two apartments there with his left hand. The second door opened.

"Where have you been .. ..?" the lady's voice trailed as she looked up to see Paul, Heidi and the bag of presents. "I was expecting the plumber. I buzzed him in ten minutes ago," she explained.

"Sorry, that was us," Paul said.

"We're looking for our daughter, Katya Schmidt. She lives in apartment seven," Heidi expounded.

"I'm sorry. We only moved here six weeks ago from

Munich. I don't know the other residents. Is she working for the Bank?" the lady asked.

"No, she's an athlete, an Olympic champion. She's lived here for two years," Heidi said.

"Oh, I thought all the Easties had left when the Bank bought the building months ago. Sorry but I can't help. Please excuse me," she said and closed the door.

"We should go to the Institute. Katya may be there," Paul said, picking up the bag of presents from the entrance hall floor.

Heidi nodded in agreement. "We'll take the train," she said.

They walked back to the main train station. An hour later, they alighted from a train in the town, five kilometres from the Institute.

"Do you remember the way to the Institute?" Heidi asked.

"I think so but I'm not certain," Paul replied.

Heidi showed the ticket collector the address and he gave directions. They walked through the light snowfall, following the trails of other footprints. Their breath puffed smokily from their mouths as the sun began to pass below the horizon. Now there was no trail to follow. Crisp snow squeaked beneath their boots; apprehension clasped their chests.

Paul recognised the building as they turned right and crunched up the drive. There was no activity, no indication of occupancy. At the main door, a chain and padlock forbade entry. Paul pressed the bell, hearing it ring inside. Heidi pointed to the windows. Jagged glass jutted from the window frames.

"It looks abandoned," Heidi said quietly.

Paul pressed the bell again, holding his thumb hard against the button for five seconds. They waited.

"There's nobody here," he agreed. "There must be

someone, somewhere on the campus," he said pensively, trying to rekindle hope.

"Yes, there should at least be a caretaker," Heidi conjoined in the raising of spirits.

For two hours, they traversed the campus. Hope ebbed as their tracks mingled only with animal spoors. Each building was padlocked, many of the windows were broken. Moonbeams on the snow lit their way.

"There's nobody here," Heidi accepted.

"Let's go back to Dresden and talk to the bank that owns the apartment," Paul suggested.

"It's too late tonight," Heidi replied, her gloved hand tugging her coat sleeve above her wristwatch. "We could stay in the town here. It will cost less and then we can take the train to Dresden in the morning," Heidi proposed.

"We may meet somebody in town who knows what has happened here," Paul concurred. "Perhaps the Institute's moved," he said.

They walked briskly back to the town as the air temperature dropped, their breaths now billowing in their wake.

They found an inn which satisfied Heidi's budgetary judgement for food and lodging. The innkeeper knew a little of the history of the Institute. He confirmed that it had closed. He didn't believe it had moved elsewhere.

"Things are changing dramatically now we are one Germany," he said. "There are elections later this month, Government departments such as the National Institute for High Performance Athletes seem to have just disappeared and even the ostmarks have been replaced with deutschmarks – all so quickly."

Heidi knew the ostmark had been replaced by the deutschmark six months earlier. She had been one of the first at the bank with their savings. The value of their nest egg had risen seven fold when converted at parity. She hadn't been aware of the other consequences of the re-unification of the Democratic Republic with the Federal Republic.

The next morning, they boarded the train for Dresden in low spirits. Their despondency was prescient. They were bounced from one bank flunkey to another and from one bank to another. Paul's demands to speak to a manager were resisted. Heidi's high horse was deftly unsaddled by a supercilious functionary.

"Madam, it is of no concern to me that I am the tenth person you have been referred to. If you listen attentively, I may be able to spare you the inconvenience of meeting an eleventh. No bank and no bank official will discuss the ownership of the bank's assets with a couple who walk in off the street in search of a missing adult daughter. Good day to you both," he clicked his heels together, bowed, turned and was gone.

"Paul, that rude, officious, little ....," Heidi fumed, searching for the final noun.

"Yes, he's all those things but he is also right," Paul determined. "We are not making any progress. We need help. I think we should go back to the village and discuss the way forward with Sylvia Mietl. Katya must be somewhere. We need a new plan to find her."

"Sylvia would know," Heidi confirmed, transferring her hope from the bank's sinking boat to a more promising craft.

Paul and Heidi surrendered to their exhaustion on the journey home, heads propped together in slumber until five minutes before their station. Paul's startled awakening jolted Heidi into consciousness.

"Where are we?" Paul asked a fellow passenger.

"A few minutes from Kelstadt," she replied.

Heidi stretched, "It will be quicker if we get a taxi to Sylvia's," she said as the train pulled into the station.

Chapter 17

SYLVIA welcomed the Schmidts into her house. She was a little perplexed that they had arrived by taxi but held her own counsel on the matter.

"Would you like a coffee or perhaps tea?" she asked as she settled Paul and Heidi on the settee.

"Coffee please," Heidi replied.

"Yes, coffee as well," Paul answered.

Sylvia returned with a coffee pot, three cups with saucers, sugar, spoons, milk and a plate of biscuits covering the floral design on the wooden tray she carried. She poured the coffee.

"Thank you," said Heidi, taking the saucer with the cup in its centre.

Paul accepted his coffee. "We've just come from Dresden," he explained.

"Oh," Sylvia exclaimed. "Cream, sugar?" she asked.

Heidi and Paul creamed their coffee and each stirred in a spoonful of sugar. As they took their first sips, "Biscuit?" Sylvia offered the plate. They both accepted. Biscuit balanced on the rim of his cup, Paul began.

"We were in Dresden searching for Katya. We haven't heard from her in five months...."

"It's not like Katya," Heidi interjected. "This is the first Christmas ever that we haven't been together."

Paul sat back in the settee, sipping his coffee as Heidi continued.

"We went to her apartment but she doesn't live there any

more. Nobody knows where she's gone. We went to the banks that apparently own the building now but they wouldn't discuss anything. They won't even confirm if they own the apartments. We went to the Institute but it's derelict; there's nobody there. Katya's disappeared and we don't know how to find her," Heidi finished, disgorging her data.

Sylvia sat considering the facts she had been given. "When did you last speak to her?" she asked.

"We had a postcard last September. She was on holiday beside a lake somewhere with her coach, Dieter Muller," Heidi replied.

"Have you had a quarrel? Have there been any arguments?" Sylvia enquired.

"No . . . . no arguments," Heidi stated, shaking her head to reinforce her answer.

"Well, Katya knows that we don't approve of her relationship with her coach," Paul added to Heidi's response.

"Do you think Katya's with her coach now?" Sylvia queried.

Paul and Heidi looked at each other, "Yes, probably, yes," said Heidi.

"I agree. I think she is with him," Paul concurred.

"Do you believe that Katya is deliberately avoiding you?" Sylvia probed.

Again Paul and Heidi looked for guidance from the other's expression. Paul responded first, "I don't think so. You know Katya as well as most. It's not in her nature to behave in such a way."

"Paul's right," Heidi agreed. "There's some circumstance or someone stopping Katya from contacting us."

Sylvia pondered what she had been told. Katya was one of her special students, one whom she held in the highest esteem. She believed Heidi and Paul were justified in their concerns.

"I can see no benefit in approaching the banks. Certainly, many of the former D.D.R. State properties have been sold. There is a bureau which has been specifically set up for this task. Even knowing the new owners is unlikely to tell us where the previous occupants have gone." Sylvia paused, looking to Heidi and Paul to accept this supposition. Heidi nodded acquiescence. Paul looked thoughtful.

"I believe the best way forward would be a letter to the new German Athletics Federation. They may have the contact details for both Katya and Herr Muller. I will draft a letter but it may be better if you send it. I will find out their postal address," Sylvia offered.

"Thank you." "Thank you," Heidi and Paul echoed, rising from the settee to embrace the retired schoolteacher.

Heidi and Paul walked back to their home carrying Katya's presents.

"I feel a little more positive, less apprehensive now that we have spoken to Sylvia," Paul declared.

Inside their cottage, Heidi placed the bag of presents on Katya's unused bed. The balm of Sylvia's involvement dissipated with the melancholy emptiness of Katya's bedroom. Heidi grasped Katya's woollen lamb comfort, Adie and soaked it with her maternal tears.

Paul sent the letter, drafted by Sylvia, to the address she gave him. Weeks passed with no response and no word from Katya. Towards the end of February, a letter arrived. The envelope was pre-printed with the name of the German Athletics Federation. Paul and Heidi sat down at the table to share their hope.

Dear Mr. Schmidt,

Unfortunately, we have no contact details for your daughter. When you do reach her, please advise her to contact the Federation as it is imperative that all elite athletes are registered. Further, we have an obligation to conduct out-of-competition doping tests.

With regard to Herr Dieter Muller, we cannot release the information you have requested as this would breach our privacy regulations.

Yours sincerely,
Gunther Kanz
German Athletics Federation

Despondence rolled down their throats, congealing in the pits of their stomachs as they absorbed the reply. A knock on the door fractured their despair. Heidi opened the door to Sylvia.

Five minutes later, coffee and cake laid out on the table, Paul passed Sylvia the letter from the Federation. She read it intently, folded it and handed it to Paul.

"I've been thinking as to the best way forward. I received a letter from a former pupil; yes, many of them still keep in touch with me," she answered rhetorically. "Where was I?" she searched her short-term memory. "Oh yes, one of my old students wrote. He has just received promotion in the Department of Social Security. I would like your permission to ask him to search for Katya's Records."

"YES," Heidi pleaded, clutching at new hope.

"Thank you," Paul said, squeezing Sylvia's right hand within his own.

"It may take a little while," Sylvia cautioned. "He isn't

supposed to do such things but I feel our relationship is robust enough to ask this favour of him."

"Should we report Katya's disappearance to the Polizei?" Paul asked.

"Yes, I think so now but it's a long shot. Missing adults, where there is no evidence of foul play, will probably not be of interest to them, even famous people such as Olympic gold medal winners."

In early April, Sylvia knocked upon the chalet door again. Her sombre demeanour forewarned Heidi and Paul as they sat with the coffee and scones.

"I am sorry but my contact can find no details since September last year. That was the last month Katya paid tax and social security. Her employer was the Institute and September is the last return they have made. There is no record of any social security payments being made to her which you would expect if she is not working."

"The Polizei have taken the details but will not investigate yet," Paul added.

"What can we do now?" Heidi pleaded.

Sylvia replied, "We will need to prepare leaflets with Katya's picture on. We must say she is missing and ask anyone with information to contact us. Keep in mind, she is an Olympic gold medallist. She is a familiar face to many in the old D.D.R. Someone, somewhere, should recognise her, know her whereabouts."

"How many leaflets? Where? How do we distribute them? Which picture of Katya should we use?" Paul's questions tumbled from his mouth.

"The picture should highlight Katya's most distinctive features, aspects that would not change, her eyes, nose and mouth," Sylvia suggested, then continued.

"Five thousand would be a good initial number to hand out in Dresden at the train stations and bus termini. Katya liked music and the theatre so we should hand out leaflets at those venues before and after performances."

Heidi felt energised by Sylvia's plan. "I will find some photos to choose from," she said, going to her bedroom.

Whilst Heidi was searching for the photos, Paul poured fresh coffee into Sylvia's cup. "Is there anything I should be doing?" he asked.

"Yes, you will need to get a telephone, a mobile phone. That will be the contact number we will print on the leaflets," she explained.

Heidi returned with some photograph albums. They chose the picture which they felt best highlighted Katya's principal features.

"I can negotiate with the printer if you wish?" Sylvia offered, "But I will need some funds. Tradesmen always seem to quote their keenest prices when paid in cash."

"Of course. How much?" asked Heidi.

"One of my ex-pupils has a small printing business. I think five hundred marks should suffice," Sylvia replied.

"When will the leaflets be ready?" Paul enquired as Heidi counted out the notes.

"We should be ready to go to Dresden in two weeks I think but I will confirm with you once you give me the mobile phone number," Sylvia said.

Heidi looked quizzically at Paul. "We need the contact phone number to print on the leaflet," he answered her puzzled face.

"I will go to Kelstadt to arrange a phone today," Paul affirmed.

Two weeks later, Heidi, Paul and Sylvia were handing out a missing person leaflet to train travellers at the Dresden Hauptbahnhof. Heidi and Sylvia appeared more skilful than Paul in interrupting the passage of potential recipients. After two hours at the train station, about half the leaflets had been handed to people.

"Let's try the bus terminus and then perhaps the main shopping area," Sylvia suggested, picking up her half-full box of leaflets.

"Ok," agreed Heidi, tucking her box under her arm.

Paul followed the lead of the two women although his box was heavier being still three-quarters full.

The bus terminus was less frantic that the train station. It was easier to obtain peoples' attention but there were less people so far fewer leaflets were distributed. In the shopping district, they positioned themselves outside the doors of the principal department store. A policeman stopped Paul and asked for an explanation of their activity. Satisfied, he wished them luck with their quest and moved on.

By early evening, they were in position in Theatreplatz where they passed out the last five hundred of the five thousand leaflets with which they had started the day. They walked to the train station at the start of their journey home.

"Whew," said Heidi, kicking off her shoes as they sat on the train.

"It's hard on the feet," agreed Sylvia, dislodging her own footwear.

"So many people today had kind words," Heidi mused. "A few remembered our Katya."

"It restores one's faith in the nature of humankind," waxed Sylvia.

"What's that sound?" Paul asked, looking about him.

"It's your mobile phone ringing," Sylvia explained.

"Oh," he uttered, scrabbling to unpocket the phone.

"Press the green button and talk," Sylvia advised.

Paul spoke into the phone, "Hello, this is Paul Schmidt."

"Yes, good, Herr Schmidt. I have one of your posters. I was at the Institute when your daughter Katya was there.

The Institute closed on the first of October and I believe your daughter went to Berlin with her coach, Herr Muller. You know they lived together I suppose?" the caller enquired.

"Yes, yes... Are you sure they went to Berlin?" Paul demanded.

"No, Herr Schmidt, I cannot be sure. This is just what I believe I heard."

"Did you ....," Paul heard the click. "Hello, hello," he pleaded but there was no answer. He passed the phone to Sylvia for confirmation.

"No, the line is not connected," she confirmed.

"Who was it? What did they say?" Heidi asked.

"It was a man who worked at the Institute. He believed that Katya went to Berlin with Dieter Muller at the beginning of October," Paul replied.

"Did he know where in Berlin?" Heidi questioned.

"No, he wasn't entirely sure that they had gone to Berlin. He thought that he had heard this was the case," Paul replied.

"Let's see what other responses we get from today," Sylvia advised.

The phone did not ring again till the next day. Over the following three weeks, Paul answered fifteen calls, mostly from people believing they had seen Katya in the past three months. A few would give no information unless they were paid a reward for their trouble first. Paul logged all the calls and, at the end of May, he went with Heidi to visit Sylvia Mietl.

Seated in her parlour, Paul summarised the responses he had received. Of the sixteen calls, three had asked for money, nine thought they had seen Katya at various locations in Dresden and three believed they had heard that she was in

Berlin. The sixteenth speculated that she had gone to Australia with Dieter Muller.

"Perhaps we should distribute leaflets in Berlin?" Heidi suggested.

"Yes, that seem sensible," Sylvia agreed.

"How do we deal with the possibility she's in Australia?" Paul asked.

"I know someone in the diplomatic service," Sylvia offered.

"Another former pupil?" Paul asked, smiling.

Sylvia returned his smile. "I can have the leaflets in a week," Sylvia said.

"Good. We will go next week then," Heidi stated, counting out five hundred marks to pay for the leaflets.

Paul and Heidi returned to their chalet. Sylvia was more dejected with the results of their campaign in Dresden than she had allowed Paul and Heidi to observe. She determined to have the death records for Dresden and Berlin checked for Katya's name.

In Berlin, they repeated the distribution formula they had used in Dresden. In addition, Paul pasted about one hundred leaflets to lampposts. Three weeks later, they had received only six calls. All of the callers asked for money.

Sylvia received a response from her contact in the diplomatic service. Enquiries had been made in Australia and Dieter Muller was living there, coaching the Australian Athletics Squad. He had been interviewed and had no knowledge of Katya's whereabouts. She was not with him and he hadn't seen her since September 1989. The Australian immigration officials had confirmed that no female had accompanied him when he entered the country.

When Sylvia gave them this news, Heidi lost control of her emotions.

"We'll never see Katya again," she yelled. "She's gone forever. She's dead," she screamed.

Paul and Sylvia clasped the distraught mother between them, holding her till she calmed.

"Katya's still alive. She's not dead," Sylvia soothed.

"How do you know?" Heidi asked defiantly.

"Because I have had someone checking the mortuary records," Sylvia said quietly. For a moment, Heidi and Paul stood in shocked silence. Tears rolled down Heidi's face, dripping from her chin as she whispered, "Then, where is she?" through gritted teeth. Her voice rose again, "Where is she? Where's our Katya? Why doesn't she contact us?"

Paul held Heidi tight in his arms to comfort her. "She may be somewhere we haven't looked," Paul contributed. "She could be in the West. She has a car so it would be easy for her to travel there," he continued, warmed by his new thesis.

"Of course," Sylvia exclaimed. "We haven't tried to trace the car. Do you have the registration number?" she asked.

"Heidi, now calmed, replied, "Yes, I have it in my address book."

Sylvia wrote down the registration number and as many of the other details as Paul and Heidi could remember.

"I will investigate the whereabouts of the car. The polizei should be able to trace it," Sylvia stated.

"We should plan to visit as many cities in West Germany as we can," Paul suggested, holding Heidi in a gentle embrace.

Through August and September, they visited Frankfurt, Cologne, Munich, Düsseldorf, Stuttgart and Hamburg. No leads to Katya's whereabouts were forthcoming. The car registration details had raised hopes but the vehicle had belonged to the State, not to Katya. It had been repossessed on the 1st October, 1990, the same day that she had been turned out of her State-owned apartment.

By autumn, the three searchers were languishing. Their hope was dissipating, crushed by the lack of any concrete leads. Paul and Heidi spent most of October and November wandering the streets of Dresden with photos of Katya. They booked out of the guest house in which they were lodging at the end of November. Heidi felt that they needed to be at the chalet in case Katya returned for Christmas. Paul needed to check the goats that Johann had been herding for him in his absence.

When they met with Sylvia in early December, she suggested a new approach to their search. "Katya may not even be in a city. She may have gone into the country."

"How do we leaflet across all of Germany?" Paul asked.

"We don't have any savings left," Heidi interrupted.

"We'll see if we can involve the media. If we could get a television company to cover her story and the mystery of her disappearance, millions of people would see it and this could identify where Katya is. Remember, she was famous once. She stood on the medal podium wearing an Olympic gold medal. Someone must know where she is," Sylvia concluded.

"Do you think you could stimulate the production of such a programme?" Paul asked enthusiastically.

"Yes . . . . Yes . . . . I believe I know who to talk to," Sylvia confirmed.

That Christmas Eve, Heidi put the presents she had bought in Munich for Katya's twenty-eighth birthday, into a cupboard with her 1991 Christmas presents. She took the other presents from Katya's bed and put them in the same cupboard. For the first time in twenty years, she knelt by Katya's bed and prayed. Katya did not come for Christmas or Sylvester. She had been missing for fifteen months.

Chapter 18

JANUARY, 1992

SYLVIA visited the Schmidts with more positive tidings. She had persuaded a television producer to feature Katya's disappearance in a programme he was filming called 'FOOTPRINTS ON THE WATER.' The programme was to examine the negative effect of the fall of the Berlin Wall on the former D.D.R. celebrities in sport, music and politics. Katya would be the case study representing sport. Sylvia enthused at the prospects for finding Katya once the production was broadcast in April. Heidi was reluctant to commit more emotional capital to new hope.

"We will just have to wait and see," she said, taking a fresh pot of coffee from the stove.

"That's great news," Paul said with conviction. "Sylvia, thank you. How can we ever repay you for all that you have done?" he complimented.

"I am very fond of Katya. I've taught many, many children throughout my life but she was really, really special," Sylvia replied, tears welling in her eyes.

Heidi's defences were breached by the teacher's distress. She had never seen Sylvia cry in the forty years she had known her. Paul wept for Katya, undone by the agitation of the two women.

"There is more good news I believe," Sylvia said, blinking the tears from her eyes. "A new law has been passed giving access to the Stasi files. As Katya's parents, you should be able to read her file. You will need to travel to Berlin. I could accompany you," she offered.

"When can we go?" Heidi pleaded, investing in new hope.

Sylvia took a letter from her purse, "I took the liberty of applying on your behalf last month," she said. "This letter arrived this morning. You have an appointment at eleven a.m. on Thursday, two days from now," she said, passing the document to Heidi.

"It says we must bring proof of identity, birth certificates, both for Katya and ourselves," she read. "I have those in my box under our bed," Heidi said, her heart now fully committed to renewed faith that she would find her daughter.

Two days later, they sat in a meeting room in Berlin. Katya's Stasi file was open on the table. Sylvia had been allowed to sit with them as their representative. An official from the bureau, responsible for the records, sat beside them to assist in areas requiring interpretation.

"The file starts in February, 1976, with a report from Herr Kutz, the village Mayor at that time, advising his Stasi handler of Katya's apparent athletic potential. The last document in the file is dated November, 1989. It is a report from Dieter Muller to his Stasi handler on a reception he had attended with Katya," advised the official, reading a note at the top of the file.

"The file finished in 1989," Heidi repeated. "But we know Katya didn't lose her apartment until October, 1990," she challenged.

"I am sorry, Frau Schmidt. All the files I have seen do not go beyond November, 1989," explained the official. "That is when the Stasi tried to destroy the files," he added. Heidi's new spirit of optimism slumped, shrivelled and was gone.

The official was discomfited by the gloom of his three

visitors. After minutes of silence he asked, "Do you wish to examine the file?"

"There might be some information that could help us find Katya," Sylvia addressed Paul and Heidi.

"Yes," Paul replied automatically.

Sylvia took the file offered by the official and read the documents in the chronological order in which they were filed. She paused at a document dated August, 1979. This break in her rhythm of reading alerted Paul.

"What is it?" he asked.

"It's a report from the Direktor of the Institute detailing the 'reactionary attitude' of Alex Durnek, Katya's coach at that time. His employment was terminated because he refused to put Katya on a programme named 'Komplex 08'."

The official interrupted. "That is the Stasi code for giving anabolic steroids and other drugs to the athletes," he explained.

Paul moved closer to Sylvia to read over her right shoulder.

"The next report in September, 1979, details the dosages of drugs Katya was given. It's signed by Dieter Muller."

Heidi broke from her trance, "Muller, Muller was giving Katya drugs. What for? What drugs? He is not a doctor," she said, moving to look over Sylvia's left shoulder.

Pages and pages of data on drugs administered to Katya followed.

"What does that symbol represent?" Sylvia asked the official.

"AI," he read. "Athlete Ignorant." It is on most of the files I have seen. The athletes were not aware that they were taking anabolic steroids. They were told that they were vitamin pills."

Paul held his head in his hands in sorrow.

"What is this entry," Heidi demanded of the official as they reached the entries in 1988.

"P-50/87, T-26/88 successful," he read. He turned the page. The report was from the doctor who had performed the abortion and the Direktor of the Institute. He quickly scan read it.

"I'm sorry," he said. "Your daughter had her baby aborted in early June, 1988 when she was twenty-eight weeks pregnant. It was an experiment to improve her ability to run faster."

"No ... No ... Noooo," Heidi screamed. "How could we let this happen to you Katya?"

Two hours later, their train left Berlin. Heidi was drowsy, her head resting on Paul's shoulder. Following her reaction to the news of Katya's abortion, the official had called for medical assistance. Now sedated, Heidi slept, relieved of the thoughts of Katya's agony which tormented her.

"She's right," Paul spoke quietly to Sylvia. "What Heidi said about us letting this happen to Katya, she's right. We should have known. We should have taken her back home in August, before Muller, when she was fifteen," he concluded.

"In many ways, it was my error," Sylvia replied. "It would have been better if you had never seen that file."

Chapter 19

BACK in the village, weeks passed before the film crew arrived. Heidi's doctor had prescribed sedatives for her. She had quizzed him on the side-effects of anabolic steroids. He had been reluctant to feed her already tortured mind with new images of Katya's potential suffering.

The television people arrived, filmed background material, interviews with Sylvia Mietl on Katya as a gifted pupil, interviews with Paul on her early training and a final interview and pleas from Heidi for news of their missing daughter.

The programme was broadcast in April. Alex Durnek saw the programme and immediately phoned the contact number shown on the television.

"Hi, who am I speaking to?" he said.

"This is Paul Schmidt," came the reply.

"Paul, my name is Alex Durnek. We have never met but, some years ago, I coached Katya when she first came to the Institute."

"I have heard Katya speak about you, Herr Durnek," Paul responded.

"I've just seen the programme on T.V. I don't know where Katya is but I would like to come to talk to you."

"Sure. Do you know where we live?" Paul asked.

"Roughly but if you could give me directions," Alex answered.

"If you take the train to Kelstadt, I can meet you at the station," Paul offered.

"Thank you but I will drive. It's easier for me. I can come tomorrow morning if that's all right with you. Perhaps we could meet at the station as it would be easy to find. I'll try to get there around eleven a.m. I'll be driving a dark green Audi. If you need to contact me for any reason, my number is

087 32 32 94."

Clutching at any glimmer of hope, Paul replied, "Thank you. It's so kind of you to make this effort for us."

"Effort, this is no effort. Katya was very special to me and to my family. I too want to know her whereabouts. If there is anything I can do to help find her, then I will," said Alex.

"I look forward to seeing you tomorrow."

Paul sat silently for a moment and then scribbled on his notepad.

"Who was that?" asked Heidi, turning from Sylvia's television set.

"Alex Durnek, Katya's old coach. He doesn't know where Katya is but would like to come from Dresden to meet us tomorrow."

"He was the coach sacked for refusing to give Katya toxins, wasn't he?" Sylvia recollected from the Stasi files.

"What was your opinion of the television programme?" Sylvia asked Heidi.

"I think it went well, don't you? Alex Durnek may be able to shed light on the activities at the Institute and that could help us get Katya back. Some people are whispering that she is dead but I don't believe she is. I'm her mother and somehow, inside me, I feel she's out there, somewhere. I hope, always hope, that Katya will come back to us," Heidi replied.

Paul's phone rang again and continued to ring each time he disconnected from his previous conversation. Twenty calls and one hour later, Sylvia offered to answer calls. Paul, grateful for the opportunity to go to the bathroom, passed the phone over as he summarised.

"Many people know Katya or know of her because of her athletic successes. Many of the calls have just been to wish us luck; none have harboured good news yet. So far, no caller has seen her since September, 1990," he finished, leaving the room.

When he returned, Heidi was animated. "The last caller believes she saw Katya in Dresden in February, '91. She thinks they worked together as cleaners in a hotel. She says Katya didn't report for work one morning and she's not sure where she went. She's given us the name of the hotel."

"I've written it down. It's the Hotel Konigstein in Pragerstrasse," Sylvia stated.

"We could go tomorrow morning," Heidi suggested.

"But Herr Durnek....?" Paul queried.

"If he's coming from Dresden, why not phone him and arrange to meet at the Hotel Konigstein instead?" Sylvia suggested.

"That's a good plan," answered Heidi.

At ten the next morning, they were drinking coffee with the duty manager of the Konigstein Hotel and explaining their quest.

"I was not here myself two years ago. I came in the summer of '91. Frau Karol looks after housekeeping and she has been here much longer than me. I will arrange for her to join you here," he said, rising from his seat in the lounge.

"Thank you for your help," Paul said, shaking the duty manager's right hand.

"Glad to be of service. The coffee is with the compliments of the house," he replied with a bow and Prussian click of his heels.

Frau Karol arrived a few minutes later. She politely refused their offer of a cup of coffee and declined their invitation to be seated. She stood at attention, feet apart, hands clasped behind her back, great bosoms straining the buttonholes of her uniform.

Sylvia told her about Katya's disappearance. Frau Karol was unmoved.

"Do you remember her?" Sylvia asked,

"Madam, I have thirty people working for me. They stay an average of fourteen weeks. I do not try to remember their names," she replied.

"So, you cannot recollect Katya Schmidt. She was quite a celebrity, an Olympic champion?" Sylvia cajoled.

"No," answered the housekeeper. Then she brought forward a black ledger she was holding behind her back and flicked through the pages. "Schmidt K left on the 18th of February after eight weeks. She was ill and taken to the hospital," she read, clamping her ledger shut.

"In what way was she ill?" Heidi asked.

"Madam, I know only what my records tell me," the housekeeper replied.

"Thank you," said Sylvia, dismissing the woman.

Paul's phone rang. "Hi, this is Alex. I am at the hotel reception desk," Alex said.

Paul's eyes traversed the entrance lobby until he saw a man standing by the reception desk, holding a mobile phone to his ear.

"I see you. I will be right over," Paul replied.

Paul returned thirty seconds later and introduced Alex to Heidi and Sylvia.

"We still have some coffee in the pot if you would like a cup?" Heidi enquired.

"Thank you, yes," Alex answered.

"Any news of Katya yet?" he asked.

"She worked here as a cleaner two years ago but she was taken to hospital," Heidi said.

"Do you know which hospital?" Alex asked.

"No, we will have to visit all the hospitals," Heidi replied.

"The closest hospital is in Friedrichstadt although there is a clinic at the main railway station," Alex offered. "I don't wish to intrude but I did want to meet you. Katya was . . . . is a special athlete. If there is anything I can do, please ask. I would love to meet her again when you find her. I leave for Barcelona in eight weeks with the German middle distance runners but I will be back the second week in August," he finished.

"That's very kind and so were your thoughts for Katya. We will keep you informed. Could you possibly ask your athletes if they have heard anything at all about Katya? We are so desperate. There must be someone, somewhere, who has an idea of where she is. We would be so grateful for any news, any information that might lead us to her," Heidi thanked Alex. Paul shook his hand.

Chapter 20

THE receptionist at the hospital in Friedrichstadt referred Sylvia's request for information on a possible patient in February, '91, to her administrator. This hospital official, while courteous and helpful, felt unable to comment concerning the medical records of an adult patient, even to her parents. No amount of pleading would alter her stated position on confidentiality. The distress this caused Heidi and Paul was evident to the bureaucrat. She consulted her computer screen, tapping out instructions through her keyboard.

"This is highly irregular but I can confirm a female patient, Katya Schmidt, was admitted on the 18th February, 1991 and discharged on the 12th of March, 1991. Date of birth, 16th October, 1963. That is it. Please, no more questions," she said, standing to signal the end of their discussion.

"Thank you," Paul said, grasping the functionary's right hand between both of his own.

They returned to the village. Paul's phone was now ringing less frequently. Within two weeks, he was lucky to receive one call a day. After four weeks, the calls stopped altogether. Heidi's initial joy at finding Katya's meagre trail had dissolved. Her mind focused on what illness might have kept Katya in hospital for three weeks.

Heidi and Paul made a few trips to Dresden, standing outside the Hotel Konigstein, talking to passers-by and hotel guests and showing them Katya's photograph. They also spent time outside the hospital in Friedrichstadt, leafleting the hospital workers.

Two weeks after their last visit to Dresden, Paul's phone rang. It was the 11th of August.

"Hi Paul. This is Alex. I am at the airport in Dresden. Please meet me in the reception area at the hospital in Friedrichstadt. I may have some news of Katya."

Two hours later, Heidi, Paul and Sylvia stepped from the village taxi which had driven them to the hospital.

"Please park and wait for us," Paul instructed Pieter Fischer, the driver.

Alex was waiting in the reception area with a nurse. "This is my sister, Theresa. She has a patient who was brought in from the railway yard two days ago. She phoned me because she believes it's Katya. I've seen her sleeping. I think it's your daughter; I think it's Katya," Alex wept as he passed on the news. Paul and Heidi cried.

"I will take you to her," said Theresa. "She's mostly been asleep. Her most serious injury is only a bump on her head but she has neglected herself and will need a lot of tenderness," Theresa advised.

Alex and Sylvia waited outside. Theresa led Heidi and Paul into the ward. Katya opened her eyes on hearing the multiple footsteps and, as she recognised the two people behind the nurse, her eyes filled with the tears that had dried up for so long. She held her face in her hands, the tears trickling through her fingers as her mother gently sat on the bed and took her in her arms. Paul's arms seemed to envelope mother and daughter, protecting them both. For five long minutes, they sat holding each other, stroking faces, caressing arms, fingertips gently exploring to confirm the reality. The tears turned to smiles and the smiles to laughter as they kissed and hugged with tear-wet cheeks, the ecstasy of the reunion consuming the trio.

116

Heidi began to drift down from her cloud. She felt the meagre muscles on Katya's skeletal frame. Her fingers traced the concavity of Katya's face, the ridges of bone beneath her receding, blue eyes. She clasped her daughter to her, holding her with gentle tenderness, stroking her hair. Paul watched through prisms of tears, a sight his soul had ached for.

Paul waved his right hand at the door, inviting Sylvia and Alex into the room. When Katya saw them, standing behind her father, her momentary confusion burst as recognition creased her face into smiles and reopened her tear ducts.

Heidi addressed Theresa, "When can Katya leave? When can we bring her home?"

"We will need to talk to the doctor but I think she can leave today," Theresa replied. "She has no clothes; we had to burn them," she cautioned.

"We can buy some new clothes now. We would be back within an hour," Heidi responded quickly.

"I will buy the clothes," Sylvia offered. "Pieter is waiting in the car park. He can drive me to a store. You stay with Katya," she said to Heidi.

At four o'clock that afternoon, Katya, dressed in her new clothes, sat in the back of Pieter's car, cuddled between Paul and Heidi. Sylvia sat in the front as the taxi left the Dresden city limits. Katya dozed against Heidi's shoulder. Paul and Heidi held hands across Katya's lap, tenderly squeezing to make certain they weren't in a dream.

Pieter dropped the Schmidts at their chalet in the valley. Sylvia was returning to the village with him. The old schoolmistress deflected Paul and Heidi's praise for her part in finding Katya and graciously accepted their gratitude.

Once inside their home, Heidi set to in the kitchen. Katya offered to help but Paul led her to the rocking chair, sat her down gently and, two minutes later, tucked a blanket about her legs.

117

"We need to replenish your strength," Heidi said, turning to Katya whose eyes had closed in slumber.

"We will have to be very patient and not create any pressure," Paul said quietly.

"I know. Many bad things must have happened. We know some of them from Berlin but we will let her talk about them only if she wants to," Heidi agreed in a hushed tone.

After supper, Katya was grateful when Heidi suggested she should go to bed. She had struggled to eat one third of the food prepared for her. In her bedroom she said, "Hello," to the loyal Adie and slipped between the cotton sheets that Heidi had dressed the bed with. She smiled through her feelings of fatigue, crumpled Adie to her breast and slept a deep, sound sleep for twelve hours.

Chapter 21

WHEN she did awake, at nine o'clock the next morning, it took Katya some moments to interpret that she was in her own bed, at home, with her parents. A tear squeezed from the corner of her eye. She lay in bed, luxuriating in the exquisite comfort. Her mind, at peace, no longer raged in remorse. After fifteen minutes of indulgence, she swung her legs over the side of the bed. Five minutes more and she presented herself for breakfast.

"I slept really well," she said, kissing Heidi on the cheek.

"Good. I've prepared some pancakes with honey and cream. There's ham and cheese, fresh bread and a jug of honeyed milk. Take whatever you wish and I won't be offended if you don't have much of an appetite," Heidi said, returning Katya's kiss.

Paul walked in from the paddock. "Morning... you're looking brighter already," he complimented, kissing the crown of Katya's head.

"I'm beginning to feel I'm alive again," Katya replied.

After breakfast, Katya walked in the farmyard, inhaled the scent of the mountains, the odour of the goats though they were in the higher pastures and listened to the sound of the ripples on the rill as it trickled through the yard. She closed her eyes, the smells and sounds of summer surrounding her senses. She could feel her mind healing.

Mornings, afternoons, evenings and nights flowed by as Katya's physical convalescence improved. Each day she walked further, either alone or in company with one or both her parents.

Heidi and Paul asked no questions. Katya told them her story when she felt the need from within. The scale of the damage to her mind and body was beyond all that they had imagined. If it is possible for a parent to increase the love they have for their child, then Paul and Heidi felt they loved Katya with a deeper intensity than that which had gone before.

Eight weeks after her return, on her twenty-ninth birthday, Katya was helping Paul drive the goats from the higher pastures when she saw a young woman sitting by a stream. Close by was a small, blue tent. One of the younger goats had wandered over to the tent to investigate. As he nibbled a wooden peg, driven into the ground to hold a guy rope, Katya hurried over.

"Is this your goat?" the woman asked pleasantly.

"Yes, his name is Oscar," Katya replied. "Have you been camping here long?" Katya enquired.

"I've been in these mountains for six weeks now," the woman replied. "I find a job, work for three or four months to earn some money, then return home to the mountains for solace," she explained.

"My name's Katya. I live with my parents in the valley over there," Katya said, pointing west.

"My name is Anya and I live wherever I am," said the woman, lyrically.

"Well, Anya, that seems to be a very Bohemian existence," Katya said jokingly.

Anya thought carefully, "I believe you're right. I am a Bohemian. That's what I am," she concurred.

"So, Anya the Bohemian, today is the anniversary of my birthday. If you wish to avail yourself of some good mountain hospitality, please come to tea this afternoon at four," Katya offered the exciting new acquaintance.

"Delighted I'll be, particularly if you give me directions to your abode," Anya responded quaintly.

Katya detailed the route, about three kilometres from where they stood. "Just follow the stream and it will be the first chalet you encounter," she said as she departed, driving Oscar in front of her.

Anya came to tea and entertained Katya with anecdotes of her unconventional approach to life. Heidi was less sure of their guest whilst Paul was almost as enthralled as Katya. Heidi softened as the universal appeal of her sugar-dusted sponge cake was confirmed by Anya's appetite for it. All of Katya's unopened presents from three years of birthdays and Christmases were brought out to be opened.

"Why haven't you opened them before?" Anya asked.

"It's a long story," Katya replied.

"Why don't you settle down?" Heidi asked Anya.

"I've done that," Anya replied. "For six years I played the flute in the Leipzig Philharmonic Orchestra," she said.

"And you don't enjoy playing the flute anymore," Heidi interpreted.

"No, there is no work anymore for flute players. The fall of the Berlin Wall marked the end of many of the D.D.R.'s orchestras. There are thousands of out-of-work musicians," Anya bowed in acknowledgement of her position amongst them.

"Well, I must go now. Thank you for your memorable, mountain hospitality," Anya said, rising to leave.

"Thank you for entertaining us," Katya replied, escorting Anya to the door.

Katya and Anya kissed each other on the cheek outside the chalet.

"How long will you be camping by the stream?" Katya asked.

"Maybe a week. Then winter's coming and the money's almost gone so I'll go back to the city to work till spring," Anya answered.

"I'll possibly see you before you go," Katya said, waving as Anya followed the stream around the mountain.

Katya met Anya three days later as she was walking past the chalet, tent tied to the top of her backpack. They chatted for twenty minutes. Anya drank a glass of fresh goat's milk.

"Good luck in the city," Katya said when Anya was leaving.

"You must come and see me. We could go to a concert if you like music," Anya offered.

"Yes, I like music," Katya replied.

"I'll write to you with an address when I have one," Anya said over her shoulder as she followed the rill to the village.

In early November, Katya went to the village with Heidi to visit Sylvia. After tea with her old teacher, Katya and Heidi strolled through the village on their way home. Thirty kisses, fifteen hugs and a proposal of marriage later, they left the village.

"Everybody was so kind," Katya said as they walked inhaling the crisp, mid-afternoon air.

"They are your people. You were born here, grew up here. They will always be here for you and they will always love you," Heidi said philosophically.

"You're right but feeling it today has given wings to my spirit," Katya eulogized.

"Would you like a cup of coffee?" Katya asked suddenly.

"Yes, when we get home," Heidi responded.

"I'll put the kettle on," Katya said, letting go of Heidi's hand.

She stretched her legs and ran towards the chalet. Heidi

122

watched her go, her heart aglow at the sight of Katya running again.

Heidi's coffee was ready when she reached home. Katya sat at the table drinking a glass of milk, Paul by her side, grinning as he cupped his mug of coffee in his hands.

The next morning, at breakfast, Katya declared her interest in running again. For the rest of November she ran alone, longer and longer distances, through the mountains, up the mountains, renewed by the sensation of power in her legs. In early December, she asked Paul if he would prepare a training programme for her. She wrote a note in her Christmas card to Alex telling him of her desire to race again.

Christmas that year was the most magical Katya could remember. The mulled wine in the village, the singing, the happiness, the painted fir cones, the shrill thrill of the children as the excitement built for the arrival of St. Nicholas. Only the adults noticed that the butcher, Hans Mandli, was absent throughout the time that the Weihnachtsmann yo-ho-hoed amongst the younger children.

The feasting at the village Sylvester Ball convinced Heidi and Paul that Katya had fully regained her appetite.

Two days into the New Year, Katya asked Paul to increase the workload in her training programme. Paul resisted, "You have to rebuild from the base. The work you are doing is sufficient for now," he advised. Katya listened, agreed, then pushed herself to run the allotted mileage in a faster time.

Paul watched, smiled, shook his head and said nothing.

At the beginning of the third week in January, a belated Christmas card arrived from Anya, the Bohemian. She had accommodation at the address she enclosed and invited Katya to a concert in Dresden on Friday, the 29th of January. Sensing Katya's excitement when she spoke of the invitation, Heidi encouraged her.

"It would be good for you to spend a few days in the city if you're sure you feel...."

"Mama, I feel great," Katya interjected, smacking a kiss on Heidi's forehead.

Paul went with the flow. "Two days rest from running would be beneficial, especially as you have increased the intensity recently," he said in support. Katya smacked a kiss on his forehead in thanks.

The visit to Dresden was a delight for Katya. She returned in high spirits.

"The concert was phenomenal," she said. "Mama, I didn't realise how beautiful classical music could be. I was floating above my seat, my mind massaged as the sounds caressed it. I was so totally relaxed," Katya effused, blue eyes glistening with exultation.

Heidi smiled at her daughter's emotional description. "It seems that you have found a new interest," she added to her smile.

"Yes.... Yes I have," Katya replied thoughtfully, then continued, "Anya was great company. She knows the city so well, the cafes, the museums, the art galleries, the best-value shops...... Almost everywhere we went cost us nothing. Even the concert tickets she was given by a friend from her old orchestra....," Katya wittered on, describing the minutiae of her time in Dresden.

Heidi listened casually, her heart happy that Katya was so content. The horrendous damage to her body and mind was healing, healing, healing.

Paul walked in to the smiles of the two women, "And what mischief are you two involved in?" he said, winking at Katya.

"Just talking about Katya's time in the city. She seems so happy. I am sure she'll go more often," Heidi grinned.

"I went running each day, only ten kilometres but it kept

me loose. It was great running through the parks and down along the river," Katya admitted.

"It's good that you run when you feel the need to," Paul accepted.

"I want to be in satisfactory condition for April," Katya said.

"That's when Alex Durnek has asked you to come to see him?" Paul confirmed as Katya nodded.

Katya continued to run longer and harder than Paul's programme demanded but her father, aware of this probability, had shortened the plan to compensate. At the beginning of April, she made her fifth visit to Dresden since January. This time, the principal reason was not a concert with Anya. She would stay overnight with Anya but she was going to see Alex. She was going to do some track work with him and discuss her future athletic career.

Chapter 22

ALEX was impressed with the progress Katya had achieved. After a timed three thousand metre run without hurdles, they went to the trackside café for a drink. Alex drank coffee, Katya, a bottle of mineral water.

"That was a very good time you ran," Alex complimented her. Katya waited, "But, as you know Katya, the closer you get to the fastest times, the smaller the improvements and the more . . . . Sorry Katya, you are aware of all of this. What is your target?" Alex asked.

"I want to be the Olympic Champion in Atlanta," Katya ricocheted her reply.

"That is as I expected. I would be honoured to train you if you wish," Alex nodded in support of his words. "Now we must look at the practicalities – Money – You will need a sponsor unless we can persuade the Athletic Federation that you are worthy of a grant," he said.

"I have sickness benefit at the moment," Katya replied.

"Good but I do not believe you will be able to receive it when you start racing. Therefore, we must make a case to the Federation and I will see which sponsors may be interested." Alex made notes on his pad.

"Next, accommodation; you will need somewhere within convenient travelling distance of this track. I think you will need to move to the city," he concluded.

"I have a friend that I stay with in the city. It is about twenty minutes by autobus to here. I am sure I can make some arrangement with her," Katya explained.

Alex nodded and ticked the accommodation heading on his notepad. "Food – It is critical that you have access to the correct diet. Your mother will not be cooking for you. This I think also involves money so I must solve that issue to ensure you eat correctly," he said, writing further notes.

"When can I start?" Katya asked eagerly.

"Whenever you are ready," Alex replied.

"Two days," Katya responded, reflectively. "I need to talk to my parents and arrange the accommodation. Yes, I think two days will be sufficient," Katya confirmed.

Heidi and Paul shared Katya's excitement. Katya's quest to prove her ability had not diminished. In her mind, the gold medal in Seoul had been negated by the knowledge that it had not been won honestly. Her parents told her they would do all that was within their capabilities to help her finish her journey.

Anya was excited for Katya. She enjoyed her company.

"You can have this room. The rent is only four hundred a month," she said when Katya told her that she needed to move to the city. "I have saved some money through the winter. I quit my job yesterday and I'm off on my travels tomorrow," Anya explained.

"Thank you," Katya responded, grateful for the room but disappointed that Anya was leaving.

The following day, Heidi and Paul helped Katya move into her new room. Anya had already left to begin her travels.

The next morning, Katya arrived at the training track, with her kitbag, at eight a.m and Alex started her on a programme of long distance training. Lap after lap she ran as Alex clicked his stopwatch after each circuit, recording her times on his notepad. After twenty-five laps, he asked her to stop.

"How do you feel?" he queried.

"Pretty good," Katya puffed back, struggling to bring her breathing under control.

"Good, you can take a break now. We will do another session after lunch at three o'clock," he said. "After your two lap warm-down, meet me in the café. What would you like to drink?" he asked.

"Mineral water is fine," Katya answered, jogging off on her warm-down laps.

Five minutes later, Katya walked into the café. She saw Alex sitting at a table in the middle of the room and walked over. She sat in a chair and picked up the bottle of mineral water, pouring the effervescent liquid into a glass with ice cubes.

Alex was drinking his coffee between chomps on a raisin-encrusted Danish pastry.

"I bought one for you," he said to Katya, pointing at the plate in the centre of the table.

"Thanks," Katya replied, picking up the sticky confection between her thumb and forefinger.

"Mmm ...... This is good," Katya complimented, licking a gooey raisin from the corner of her mouth. "Alex, what happened at the Institute in August, '79? One day you coached me and the next day you had gone. Nobody was willing to talk about you. There were some wild rumours of impropriety with one of the young girls but we didn't believe that," Katya explained.

Alex rubbed the tips of his third and fourth fingers across the centre of his forehead. He inhaled, exhaled and began his answer.

"I was sacked by the Direktor. He gave me one hour to agree to put you onto a regime of anabolic steroids. I discussed our position with Mika. She agreed that we could not sacrifice you or anyone else for the sake of our own comfortable lifestyle. We were escorted from the campus that evening. Our possessions were removed from our apartment and left in the street. We stayed with Mika's parents for two days until the Stasi arrived. They accused Mika's father of harbouring a subversive. They threatened him, said they would arrest him. I spoke to Mika's father very rudely and stormed out of the one-roomed studio. This ruse worked because the Stasi left shortly afterwards without my father-in-law. I waited a few hours and then went back into the studio. We talked and eventually Mika agreed to stay with her parents and look after Anna who was only fourteen months old at the time.

I went to look for work and accommodation and then Mika and Anna were to follow me once I was established. It took me eighteen months to find permanent work. Mika came with Anna and we lived in a hut in the forest where I was working as a woodcutter. We stayed seven years. Anna was ten years old when we came back to Dresden. Mika taught her at home in the woods because we didn't want to risk enrolling her in a local school. The Stasi had their people everywhere but when the Berlin Wall fell, so did their power. After re-unification, I applied to the new German Athletic Federation for a post as a trainer. Luckily, they found my Stasi file which confirmed I had not been involved in 'Komplex 08'."

"What is Komplex 08?" Katya interrupted.

"It's the Stasi code name for the systematic doping of athletes with anabolic steroids and other chemical formulae," Alex stated. "When I left, I did have very mixed feelings because I could have tried to thwart Komplex 08 if I'd stayed but I knew that I didn't stand a chance in fighting State directives. I did feel very guilty walking away from you and I still do. I know what I did, I had to do for my own sanity and beliefs but, in walking away, I did leave you and Brigitte behind at the Institute."

"My mother told me that I was given drugs, Alex. She read a report from Dieter Muller in my Stasi file. He told me he was giving me vitamin tablets but he lied."

Alex's head slipped into his hands and he hunched over the table, running his fingers slowly, methodically through his hair, silent for a while.

"Alex, I'm sorry I interrupted. Please tell me the rest of your story," Katya apologised.

"Katya, since I left the Institute I have been in knots because, in walking away, I knew I was leaving you in a vulnerable situation. I had hoped that the Direktor would be shocked by my actions and then question what he and the State were doing but, realistically, that was never going to be the case. I actually don't know what else I could have done at the time and I had to safeguard my family; the State is a formidable enemy. The fact that you were given steroids, the fact that athletes such as Brigitte Meinhof actually died..."

Alex paused, his head sinking deep into hands again. Katya leaned forward, placing her hand on his. Alex gathered his thoughts, raised himself up to look directly into the blue eyes he had never allowed himself to forget. His voice breaking, he said, "I will never ever be able to forgive myself..."

Katya held his hands tight and whispered, "You did what was right at the time. You did the only thing in your power to do at the time. There was nothing else you could have done. What the Direktor, Dieter and the other coaches who remained at the Institute did was unforgivable. They should be prosecuted for what they have done. What you did, Alex, was right."

Alex looked up, a tear escaping from his eye; he hurriedly wiped it away. Katya smiled, "Please tell me the end of your story."

Alex breathed in deeply, "I'm sorry, Katya."

"Alex, please, you found me. You have given me my life

back again; you have nothing to be sorry for. It is me who cannot thank you enough for being with me now. Now please, tell me the end of your story."

Alex smiled and continued, "Okay then, well, I'd almost finished actually. The Federation gave me a position training the men's middle distance runners. Some of my athletes were selected for the Barcelona Olympics. Now, tell me what happened to you after I left the Institute?" Alex asked.

Katya related her history for the next thirty minutes. Alex's brow creased more and more as he listened to the horrors which had been perpetrated on Katya and the later consequences.

When she had finished her spoken biography, Alex asked, "Why do you want to compete again in Atlanta?"

"Because I didn't win in Seoul. Now that I know the regime I was on, I know it was not an honest competition," Katya replied.

Alex looked at his watch. "It's lunchtime already," he said, ruffling Katya's hair. "Let's go and get some spaghetti with meat-balls."

Katya trained three times a day, six days a week, Sunday being her rest day. As her endurance increased, so too did the severity of each session. Alex introduced her to a nutrition expert. Katya's body became a fuel-burning machine and her speed over three thousand metres increased.

In early August, she ran her first competitive race, winning the German National Championship Steeplechase in a time forty seconds slower than that which she had achieved in Seoul.

"Well done," Alex said, congratulating her at the end of her race.

"What was my time?" Katya asked.

"Nine forty one," Alex replied.

Katya screwed up her nose in disappointment.

"The time's fine. You've only been in serious training for sixteen weeks. The Olympics are still three years away," he counselled.

The following Monday morning, Alex told Katya that she was now considered to be an elite category athlete and, as a result, the German Federation would pay her four thousand marks per month. He has also managed to get one of the city banks to sponsor her for a similar amount. Katya was elated. She could now buy a car and move to a two bedroom apartment, overlooking the park. Her parents would have somewhere to stay when they came to visit.

Heidi and Paul came to the city in September to help find the apartment. Two weeks later, they returned to help with her move to her new address.

"The view is so much …… " Heidi said, hesitating.

"Better," Katya confirmed. "It is more tranquil. I can run straight into the park with only the one road to cross," Katya enthused.

"Your training must be going well," Paul said. "You look much stronger," he added.

"I am," Katya responded.

"Let's go to a restaurant for dinner," Katya declared, adapting to her new-found solvency.

The running and weight-training sessions continued throughout October. At the end of that month, Anya returned.

"They gave me your forwarding address at our last digs," she explained as Katya delightedly yanked her into the flat.

Anya stayed until the following March when, once again, she left for the mountains. Katya was sad for a week after she left but her training soon began to blunt her emotions. As she became stronger and fitter, she also became more and more fatigued. From April through July she trained, she ate, she slept, she trained, she ate, she rested, she trained, she ate, she slept, each day except Sunday. On Sundays, she ate and when not eating, she was resting or sleeping.

At the European Championships in Helsinki in August, she placed last of the twelve runners in the final. Katya was distraught. Alex led her from the trackside.

"We'll analyse the race in the morning," he said.

Next day, after breakfast, they talked. "I am not concerned by this result," Alex said. Katya did not respond. "We discussed the likely outcome of the race before the start. You have to rebuild after three years out of training. Your laps were consistent. It's the pace you are lacking but we will work on that in eighteen months. First we must rebuild, then improve on your endurance base."

"I believe in you. I accept what you say," Katya said.

"But," Alex added, "You were going to say but.... What is the but?" he asked.

"This is the first international race that I have run clean and I am last," Katya said quietly.

"Katya, if you want speed now, you must sacrifice endurance. To win the Olympics, we must build the endurance base and then build the speed. Your time yesterday was five seconds faster than you ran last year to win the National Championships," Alex stated.

"Okay," Katya acknowledged.

Chapter 23

ALEX continued with his base-building programme through the autumn, through winter into spring.

Anya returned in October and left for the mountains again in March. April, May and June passed. Katya's legs felt as if they had run around the world.

At the end of June, Alex told her that he did not want her to race at the World Championships. Instead, she would continue with her base-building programme; this had increased in intensity twice since the Europeans in Helsinki. Now, it would increase again. Katya's body screamed with fatigue. Her brain gave automatic instructions to her legs, her feet, her arms – run, push, lift, on the track, in the gym, through the park, a blur of work, work, work.

Anya was back. She tried to understand Katya's permanent lethargy. She took her to concerts on her Sundays off but, whereas the music before had inspired Katya, it now relaxed her into slumber. Anya talked to Alex, expressing her concern for her friend's health.

"She's not sick," Alex said. "She's just tired, extremely tired. It's the price she must pay to become a champion. It's the price all her serious competitors are paying right now."

Anya didn't understand. What drives Katya she wondered but, inwardly, she had pride in her friend's tenacity.

March came and Anya stayed. For four weeks, Katya's training workload was reduced by sixty per cent. She recovered with vigour. She spent evenings wandering the city with Anya, a melee of concerts, restaurants, cinemas and cafes. Her body began to feel lighter. With every step she took, she sprang from the ground.

She won the selection race to represent Germany in the Atlanta Olympics by over half a lap. Training sessions were now shorter, more dynamic, concentrating on speed. Katya now worried that she was not training enough.

Alex smiled, "You're fine. I want you to run a full time trial two weeks from now."

Heidi and Paul came more frequently to visit Katya and, most weekends, Katya drove Anya to her parents' chalet for Sunday lunch.

Katya invited Heidi, Paul and Anya to spectate at her time trial. Alex talked to Katya as she stripped off her tracksuit alongside the other club athletes.

"I have arranged pacemakers. Each will run one thousand metres with you, then drop out and the next girl will start. Have you any questions Katya?"

"No, thanks, Alex. I'm fine. Let's get going," Katya smiled, belying the nervousness she felt inside. She lined up beside the first pacemaker. "Thanks for helping me," she whispered as they looked down the track.

"It's a pleasure," her pacer whispered back, patting her gently on the back. Alex moved into position alongside.

"Get ready," he called and then fired the start gun, pressing the button on top of his stopwatch simultaneously.

Nine minutes and five point two seconds later, he pressed the button again. Katya jogged one lap after she had finished, then joined the small throng around Alex.

"Well done," he said. "Nine five. That's the second fastest time ever for the Women's Steeplechase."

Katya nodded, tears welling. She had run nine minutes one second in Seoul. She knew she had a chance to prove she was a true champion. She looked at Heidi, Paul and Anya standing beside Alex. The most important people in her life would be there to witness it.

Chapter 24

ATLANTA, JULY, 1996 WEDNESDAY

FLAGS, banners, posters and even more flags were displayed in every direction. Katya's eyes wandered. The emblems of the Atlanta Olympics and the national colours of all the participating nations created a confusion of colour. The arrivals hall was dressed with drapeaux ten metres long. The smiling faces of the liveried volunteers proclaimed their eagerness to welcome the German team to their city.

Katya's memory was engaged. Eight years ago, a quarter of her lifetime, she remembered Seoul had put on such a show. Then the D.D.R. team were too inhibited to absorb the spectacle; she was too inhibited. Closing her eyes, Katya promised herself to savour every moment this time. She still wanted victory even more than before. She determined to prove to herself that she was the best athlete in her event, not just a successful cheat. This time, she would take a full part in the Olympic celebration and become a true Olympian. She would immerse herself in all that this entailed by honouring her hosts, by honouring her fellow competitors, by giving of her best in competition and with no cheating. Yes, this time, she would ensure it was different.

Her eyes opened, sparkling with excitement. Katya grabbed the person closest to her and smacked a kiss on his cheek, her arms about him squeezing the air from his lungs. Otto Brun, the seventeen year old gymnast, returned both hug and kiss spontaneously and then, scarlet-faced, unwrapped the embrace.

Katya boarded the coach to the accreditation centre. Two hours later, she boarded another coach to take her into the Olympic Athletes' Village. The pass, which displayed her photographic identification and status as an athlete, hung on a heavy weave ribbon between her breasts. This document, sealed in plastic, was her passport for entry into the Athletes' Village, the Athletics Stadium and the Opening Ceremony which would take place in the Athletics Stadium.

The Olympic Athletes' Village was as secure as any military base, possibly more so. Katya held her pass up to the hand-held scanner and the security official nodded acceptance. She moved forward, through the airport-style metal detecting frame, into the village.

A German team official indicated Katya's room number and the names of her three room-mates, Silke Dietz, Holga Lange and Katryn Kolbe. Katya knew Silke, the ten thousand metre runner and Katryn, a long jumper. Holga was on the team for the first time having unexpectedly won the national trials in the javelin. Katya met Silke in the apartment allocated to them. Their luggage was already in the room. Four large kitbags containing their official uniforms had been placed in the centre of the room. Each was named with a marker pen. Having chosen their beds, Katya and Silke started to examine the contents of their kitbags.

"What do you think of the colour?" asked Silke, her wrinkled nose a hint of the answer she expected as she held up the russet-shaded skirt to be worn at the Opening Ceremony.

"It's not too bad," replied Katya, holding the green jacket against the skirt. "The contrast works and the shades compliment each other," she added.

"Yep, of course you're right," replied Silke. "Let's hope they've got the sizing right," she finished, pulling her sweater over her head. The official uniforms lay in two heaps by their beds as Katya and Silke, in brassieres and panties, undid the buttons on their Opening Ceremony blouses in order to try them on.

The apartment door burst open as Katryn Kolbe crashed in.

"Sorreeee...," she exclaimed, pretending to exit in embarrassment. "I don't want to be a gooseberry," she continued, devilment writ in the expression on her face.

"Come in. Close the door you twit," said Silke, her smile welcoming the long jumper.

"Are these the outfits from the famous fashion house," quipped Katryn, humping the kitbag with her name on it onto one of the two, free beds.

"Must be unsold stock," said Silke, still unconvinced of the merits of the outfit.

"Wow, it looks great on you," Katryn addressed Katya.

"It's her long, blonde hair. The green highlights it," said Silke, adjusting her own jacket in front of the mirror. "My auburn hair doesn't quite do the same," intoned Silke, twirling, looking over her shoulder at her back in the mirror.

"Red," barked Katryn.

"More russet than red," replied Katya, her hands smoothing her skirt over her thighs.

"No, red, not auburn. Silke's hair is red," stated Katryn, holding the waist of her own russet skirt which she had pulled from her kitbag.

"Aub...," Silke's reply was drowned by the shriek from Katryn.

"Shit, shit, it doesn't fit," she yelled, thumbs either end of the waist, stretching the width. She dropped the skirt and pulled on the green jacket. As her hands disappeared from view and her knees challenged the jacket hem, Katya recommended that Katryn should go and see the team manager.

"It's a mistake. They are bound to have the right size for you."

"Take the kitbag with you," Silke added helpfully, the slur on her hair colour forgotten.

Katryn returned half an hour later with a new, unnamed kitbag and dropped it unopened on her bed.

"She's not coming. She didn't travel," said Katryn, mysteriously. Silke winked at Katya. They had both roomed with Katryn before. She wasn't to be encouraged so they both continued to put their clothes in the closets. Exasperated, Katryn squealed, "There will only be the three of us in here. The team manager told me that Holga Lange has been left at home. Her last test was positive. She...," a knock on the door interrupted Katryn. The team manager apologised for disturbing them, picked up the kitbag with Holga Lange's name on it and left, closing the door quietly.

"She tested positive on both samples although, apparently, she claims she didn't take steroids," Katryn concluded.

"She will miss her first Olympics and she's thirty-six years old now so what chance will she have for Sydney in four years. She will be forty," said Silke, thoughtfully.

"It's a pity but she has tested positive whatever her claims of innocence," Katryn replied.

"Yep, they always claim to be innocent. I can't remember any athlete admitting they took performance enhancers," Silke rejoined as her sympathy for Holga waned.

"What's your view Katya?" Silke continued. "You competed for the D.D.R. when they were using steroids," Silke concluded, her eyes locked on a freckle on her knee, signalling her embarrassment.

Katya waited, her eyes on the auburn crown of Silke's head. Her silence caused Silke to look up, to look into Katya's eyes. Katya's response began, "I think it is possible that she is innocent. It is possible that drugs have entered her body without her consent or knowledge but now she is tainted; she would not be competing fairly so it is right that she is not here."

"But ..." Katryn butted in.

"I think the coincidence," Katya continued, overriding Katryn's interjection, "of the dramatic improvement in her personal best throws this season, especially when she was competing for many seasons at a lower level, suggests she started to take steroids through last winter." Katya finished her judgement.

"Mmm, it's often the ones who leap up the world rankings unexpectedly that later test positive," Silke concurred.

"Silke, you also asked for my views on the D.D.R. system," said Katya.

"No, no, it's fine. I didn't mean to ...," stumbled Silke.

"It's okay Silke. I don't have a problem talking about it," rejoined Katya. "It's pretty well documented that the D.D.R. sports training programme included the systematic use of steroids and masking agents which were banned by the International Athletics Federation and the International Olympic Council. Discovery of the use of these performance enhancers at the time of competition would have led to the disqualification of the competitor. I was part of the programme but I was completely unaware of the nature and purpose of the pills I was taking. During my running career as a D.D.R. athlete, I didn't know I was on steroids although, towards the end, when I was twenty-two years of age, the secrecy of our programme felt wrong," Katya paused. "Maybe I am not explaining this very well but my gut instinct was that something was somehow wrong but I didn't know what. I felt that things were not necessarily as presented to us by our trainers but I didn't know why not. I wanted so much to trust them because they were my means to an Olympic medal but, in my heart, I knew their behaviour was furtive at times. At international meets, our access to non-team members was strictly controlled but we still got the feeling that other competitors didn't trust us," Katya looked to Katryn and then back to Silke, their slight nods confirmation that they understood what she was saying. Katya continued, "I did nothing to confirm or deny my feeling of unease. I acquiesced, happy not to rock the boat, content to run and win. I did receive a gold medal in Seoul but I did not win. I was a cheat. I have no pride in the result, only shame," Katya concluded, a tear meandering down her cheek. Silke moved from her bed and hugged Katya.

"You're too hard on yourself. I remember the sensation your race caused. You won by ten seconds and took five seconds off the world record," Silke comforted.

Katryn now knelt at Katya's feet, holding her hands. "Thank you, thank you both," said Katya, squeezing Katryn's hands, leaning into Silke's hug. "I dream sometimes that it was different, that our sporting records were the result of a better understanding of technique, diet, training programmes and recovery methods. Since the end of the D.D.R., our coaches and trainers have dispersed across the globe, helping athletes from other nations to become champions. If only our programme had stayed within the rules and used science but not chemicals. If only .... but .... but it didn't. My Olympic gold medal was gained by cheating, valueless, taken from another athlete who deserved to stand on the top of the podium not below me. She did not deserve to see her country's flag below my own; she ran clean. She earned the right to hear her national anthem, see her flag raised highest as an acknowledgement that she was the best in the world. That is the spiritual nirvana for most competitors." Katya finished calmly, excused herself and went to the bathroom.

Chapter 25

THURSDAY, 8.00 AM

THE morning after Katya's arrival in the village, she boarded the athletes' bus for the training track. Alex sat in the seat beside her.

"Did you wake early?" he asked.

"About four thirty," replied Katya. "I was so tired, I went to bed at about nine o'clock and slept soon after."

"You have a six hour time difference to adjust to. It's two p.m. in Dresden right now," he said, looking at his watch. "Your body should be fully adjusted by the final a week tomorrow. The final is scheduled for eleven a.m., provided the women's javelin finishes on time. So, leaving the village at about this time is ideal but try to go to bed a little later. Four thirty is a bit too early to wake; around six would be ideal. Breakfast should be finished by seven forty so that we can be on the bus by eight. We'll get to the stadium by about eight thirty but, if the rumoured transport problems materialise and the security checks slow things down, we should still get there by nine thirty giving you plenty of time to warm up and race at eleven," Alex finished, realising he was talking to himself as Katya's sleeping head rested upon his shoulder.

As the bus arrived at the training track beside the stadium forty-five minutes later, Alex eased his shoulder upwards to awaken Katya. It took fifteen minutes for their accreditation to be checked, kitbags x-rayed and bodies scanned by metal detectors in the security check queue.

Katya worked through her stretching routines and then started her track work. The long distances had been run. Alex worked on her speed. They practiced, firstly increasing her pace and then finishing with a few strides and jumps, landing right foot on the track beyond the heavy, wooden hurdles.

Satisfied with the session, Alex told Katya he had to leave for the team captains' meeting. This dealt with the organisation of the athletic events, changes to schedules, feeding, transport and provision of air-conditioning for the athletes. "What time do you want to go into the gym?" he asked Katya.

"I will get some lunch here," said Katya. "I have a media appointment at four o'clock this afternoon and I would like to go to the flag raising ceremony first, if that's possible," she stated.

"How about five thirty or six then?" Alex queried.

"Five thirty sounds good," she answered.

Katya sat at the table, eating her bowl of pasta twirls and gazing round the athletes' canteen.

"May I sit here?" asked an Indian girl, putting down her plastic tray beside Katya.

"S...sure...sure," replied Katya, hand over her mouth as she swallowed the last mouthful of pasta.

"My name is Sudha Lall," said the Indian girl.

Katya responded, "Hi Soda, my name is...,"

"Katya Schmidt," cut in Sudha. "You're really famous. Everyone knows you and, by the way, it's Sud...ha," said Sudha, pointing to her name on her accreditation card. "I am representing India in the three thousand metre steeple chase for which you, Katya, are the favourite to win and I, the favourite to be last in the first heat," Sudha stated authoratively.

"Well, it seems easier for you to confirm your prediction for yourself rather than the target you've set me," said Katya, smiling.

"Oh no, I must not," cried Sudha.

"Must not what?" enquired Katya kindly.

"I must not come last. It would bring humiliation upon my country, upon my family," Sudha replied.

"Why?" Katya asked.

"Because it is not usual for an Indian lady to be seen in such competition. In my family it is not considered to be seemly. My mother and grandmother determined that I should not be a runner. In almost all instances, their judgement is final. My good fortune was to have my father champion my cause. He spoke forcefully in my favour. He, himself, had been an Indian national champion at running although he had never raced in the Olympics, much to his regret later in his life. He was to train me here but he is sick and could not travel. If I come last, it will confirm the prejudices. You are a European. It must be difficult to understand that, in many countries, women are not allowed to enter the Olympic Games," Sudha spoke with earnest conviction, her eyebrows meeting above her nose as she delivered her explanation.

"I am sorry," Katya apologised. "I have never given any thought to such a problem. My father was also a champion runner and he trained me. My mother supported me too. If I can help you in any way, please tell me," Katya offered.

"It is me who must apologise. It was very bad mannered of me to lecture you so. Thank you for your kind offer of assistance but I have detained you too much already. I will truly pray that your quest at the Championship is successful," Sudha rose to leave as she finished speaking.

"Sudha, train with me tomorrow morning - nine thirty a.m. here," Katya said emphatically.

"Are you sure? That would be brilliant. Thank you, thank you so much," Sudha responded breathlessly.

"Are you going back to the village now?" Katya asked.

"Yes," replied Sudha.

"Then let's travel back together," said Katya.

On the coach, returning to the village, Sudha quizzed Katya, "How intrusive are the media?" she asked.

"As little or as much as you allow," Katya replied. "This is the best venue in the world for ensuring the privacy of the athletes," she continued. "All media must get access passes from the team officials to enter the village and their behaviour, once inside, is strictly regulated."

"But the demands to see you must be so high. Even the Indian papers are interested in your astonishing story," Sudha stated.

Katya smiled at the innocent earnestness of the young girl from India. "When we arrived here, there were over three hundred requests from the media. I discussed the situation with my coach, Alex, who you'll meet tomorrow and the team management. It was agreed that whilst I'm competing, I will take three interviews of up to one hour each, one today, one next Wednesday after the semi-final and the third one on Friday, after the final," Katya concluded as the bus arrived in the village.

"Good luck with today's interview then," said Sudha as they parted.

"Thanks. See you tomorrow," Katya responded.

As Katya opened the door of the apartment, Silke, dressed in her formal team uniform, was about to leave.

"I thought you wanted to go to the flag-raising ceremony?" Silke asked as she passed Katya.

"I do, I do," Katya replied. "What time is it?" said Katya,

pulling off her track suit top, stumbling as she tried to untie her trainers whilst moving to the bathroom.

"The ceremony starts in about thirty minutes, at three, but we have been asked to assemble outside here in five minutes to form an echelon and march to the flagpole arena," Silke replied. "If you hurry, I will wait for you," Silke offered.

"Ess pleas," replied Katya, applying her lipstick.

Five minutes later, Katya and Silke were outside with the other members of the German team. They had volunteered to represent their country at the raising of the black, red and yellow German flag. This signified the team's presence in the Olympic Village.

After the short ceremony, Katya left for the interview area, set aside for media visits. Christoph Kleim, the team manager, accompanied her. He would supervise the entry and exit of the visitors and also, their behaviour in the village. Katya felt confident in his company. He appeared to say and do little though he achieved much. Few operational problems arose and when they did, he dealt with them quietly and quickly.

Katya interacted easily with this comfortably competent team official.

"Who are we seeing?" she asked as they entered the interview area. Faces raised in recognition as a melee of journalists waited to interview numerous athletes. There was no scrum of shouted questions or flashing cameras; they knew the rules and they obeyed them.

"Newsweek, nothing controversial, questions first, then a short photo-shoot," said Christoph easily, the delivery of each word lapping like warm water, soothing the feet. "Good morning gentlemen. This is Katya Schmidt and I am Christoph Kleim," he said, shaking the hands of the two men standing before them. They exchanged handshakes, a knitting pattern of crossed arms.

"Good to meet you Katya," said the taller of the two men, confidently.

Katya turned from the shorter man. He was wearing denim jeans, a white t-shirt and a bulging, unbuttoned, khaki waistcoat. His camera, a third eye, bumped against his abdomen.

The taller man addressed her, "My name is Harry Peters. I will be interviewing you," his smile bright enough to sell whatever brand of toothpaste he used, Katya's mind giggled. Harry Peters, perplexed at the amusement in Katya's smile, continued, "This is Paul Laver, our cameraman," he said, nodding in the direction of the three-eyed man. Katya nodded her head, turning towards the cameraman. "So, to business," said Harry, rubbing his hands together. "Do you mind?" he addressed Katya, holding out a small tape recorder. Katya nodded assent. "Good," said Harry, depressing a button on the side as they sat down opposite each other. Harry placed the recorder on the coffee table between them, drawing his chair closer. Katya's nose twitched as the odour from Harry's aftershave invaded her nostrils. "You okay to begin?" asked Harry, aware of some distraction. Katya nodded assent again. "Jees," Harry thought, thinking how he would get Katya talking. "How was your flight out here? How long did it take?" he asked.

"It was fine. The food was good. My seat was comfortable and I slept for four of the eight hours, so overall, I had a good flight, thank you. Lufthansa is a good airline," Katya concluded with a commercial plug for one of the companies that sponsored her.

"Are you pleased with the welcome you have received in Atlanta?" Harry asked.

"Yes, it's been great. The people have been very friendly, very warm," Katya responded.

"What do you think of the facilities in the village?" Harry asked on autopilot but professional enough to sound sincere and interested.

"I think the accommodation is excellent. The food on offer in the cafeteria is great, plenty of variety and good quality," Katya replied, glancing at Christoph who was engaged in his own conversation with Paul, the photographer. Christoph, attending both to his own conversation and the interview, winked encouragement at Katya.

"You are joint favourite for the womens' three thousand metre steeplechase with Shannon Whelan-Myers. It's a re-run of Seoul. What do you think of your chances this time?" Harry enquired, now honing in on the substance of his interview.

Christoph, smiling, shook his head, a signal to Paul that their conversation had finished. He turned in his chair to face Katya who was replying to Harry's question.

"There are many athletes with a chance. I wouldn't categorise this as a two woman race," Katya replied, reflectively.

"Oh, who would you consider to be your most serious challengers?" Harry asked.

"Well, there are probably twelve to fifteen possible medallists. Ileana Donat, the Romanian, has a good record this season. The Chinese woman is reputed to be fast..."

"What's her name?" Harry interjected.

"Chen Zhiming," Katya responded.

"Any others?" asked Harry.

"Sure, the Kenyans, Joyce Keino and Rose Biwatt will be very good. Kim OK-Kyung of Korea ran a fast time four weeks ago. There's probably at least another half dozen plus the surprise," Katya concluded.

"What do you mean, the surprise?" Harry queried.

"In every major championship, there are always one or two who perform well above their previous best times. There are forty-three entries so the surprise could be any one or two from those I haven't mentioned," said Katya.

"Is this the first time you have raced Shannon Myers since the Seoul final?" Harry asked.

"Yes," Katya answered.

Harry coughed into the palm of his hand, "Katya, can you expand on that? Why do you think you haven't raced each other? Have you both been avoiding each other?" Harry pressed.

"No, we haven't been avoiding each other. As you may know, I have only started racing again in the past three years. Shannon has not raced every season as she has been pregnant. It's a coincidence, nothing more but we will race together this week," Katya stated.

"Thank you, Katya," said Harry, rising, hand out-stretched. Katya rose and shook the proffered right hand.

"Katya, can we take a few shots?" Paul asked.

"Sure, where do you want me?" Katya responded.

"Just over there, by that banner with the Olympic rings," Paul replied, pointing to the spot he had previously chosen whilst Katya was being interviewed. Katya moved to the spot indicated by Paul. Paul pressed his camera to his face.

"Good, good, Katya. Just a little left so I can get all the rings in," said Paul through the half of his mouth not squashed by his camera. "Great, great," he said as he took four pictures click, click, click, click, the shutter opening and closing. "Katya, could you take your jacket off, hold it in your right hand, sling it across your shoulder?" Paul asked. Katya followed his direction. "Good, good, smile Katya. Great, great." Click, click, click, three more pictures were taken. Christoph Kleim patted Harry's shoulder, reached out and shook his hand.

"Thank you," he said, firmly. Paul lowered his camera and shook Christoph's hand.

"Thank you, gentlemen," Christoph said, looking at his wristwatch.

"Katya, I believe you have a training session to attend."

"Yes," said Katya, shaking hands with first Paul and then Harry.

"We'll do a good piece, Katya. Good luck with the racing," Harry said as he let go of Katya's hand.

Katya hurried back to the apartment to change into her kit for her gym session. Silke and Katryn were lounging on their beds when she entered.

"How was the interview?" Katryn asked.

"No problems," Katya summed up. "I'm going to do a gym session. Have you done yours yet?" Katya asked.

"Yes, we've just come back," Silke replied.

"See you later then," Katya said, exiting in her tracksuit and trainers.

At the door, Katya stopped, "What time are you having dinner?" she asked.

"How long will you be?" Silke responded.

"I should be back in an hour, by six thirty," Katya replied.

"We'll wait for you," Silke stated, answering for the mute Katryn.

Alex was waiting when Katya arrived at the gymnasium.

"It's very busy here," he said, meandering through the athletes strewn across the floor, twisting, bending and stretching on their blue exercise mats.

Katya smiled inwardly as they passed a group of sprinters chatting to each other, occasionally lifting a bar laden with large weights, then checking their muscle definition in the floor-to-ceiling wall mirrors.

"What's amusing you?" Alex queried, noticing Katya's smile. Katya looked towards an athlete wearing shorts, torso bare, turning to look in the mirror. "Oh," Alex responded. "Yes, a gym session for the explosive events is a lot different to the requirements of the endurance racers," he said.

Forty-five minutes later, soused in her own sweat, Katya left the gym to shower at the apartment.

"Eight tomorrow morning, at the bus station," Alex said as they walked from the gymnasium.

"Eight it is," Katya replied. "Oh, Alex, I have invited Sudha Lall to train with us tomorrow. She'll meet us at the track at nine thirty. Is that alright?" said Katya.

"Fine, see you at eight," Alex replied, thoughtfully.

Chapter 26

SILKE followed Katryn and Katya as they looked for a vacant table on which to place their laden trays. Katryn squeezed between occupied plastic chairs to the end of a table which had six vacant places at the far end. She smiled a greeting at the Japanese and Italian athletes who shifted their chairs to ease her passage. Once in possession of their seats, the three unloaded their trays.

"It's a fantastic selection of food," said Silke.

"For now, I'll keep away from the cakes and pastries but when I've finished racing...," Katya left her sentence unfinished.

"I will be right beside you," Silke said, laughing.

"Focus, focus, that's what you two need to do. This is the Olympic Games," Katryn admonished. "Hey, look at the butt on that Russian," she continued, pointing at an athlete wearing a blue, white and red tracksuit top with the word RUSSIA stretched across his back.

"FOCUS, FOCUS," Katya and Silke said, giggling in unison.

"When are you competing?" Katya asked Silke, moving the conversation away from men-spotting.

"Next Wednesday is the heat. Then, if I qualify, the final is at 6.00 p.m. on Saturday," Silke replied.

"My qualification round is Friday. I'm in pool B and the final starts at 1.00 p.m. on Sunday," Katryn stated. "When are your races?" asked Katryn, looking at Katya who sat on the opposite side of the table, facing her.

"The first round is on Monday morning, the semi-final on Wednesday afternoon and the final on Friday morning," Katya said.

"So, the cakes will take a severe battering a week on Monday then," said Silke, impishly.

Katya yawned, "I'm feeling the time difference now," she said.

"What time is it at home?" Katryn asked.

"Well it's almost eight p.m. here," said Silke, looking at her wristwatch. "So, that makes it close to two a.m. in Germany," she concluded.

"I must try to stay awake for another couple of hours then," Katya said, yawning again. "I don't want to wake at four thirty tomorrow morning," she added.

"I've got a good book that I finished on the flight if you're interested," Silke offered.

"We could wander round the village, check out the new arrivals," Katryn suggested.

Silke looked at Katya whose hand was raised to her mouth to hide another yawn. "FOCUS, FOCUS," they shouted playfully at Katryn.

"Well, you go and read your books and I'll go and mingle. Forming international friendship is part of the Olympic ethos you know," she stated, frowning to add gravitas to her pronouncement.

"Don't wake us up if you're back late then," Silke pleaded.

"See you in the morning if I'm not lucky," Katryn said, cheekily waving as she set out to mingle. Katya and Silke returned to their apartment.

Chapter 27

FRIDAY

NEXT morning, Alex and Katya stood in line for forty minutes, waiting for a bus to take them to the training track. They arrived at nine twenty. Sudha was already waiting there. Katya introduced her to Alex.

"Join in with Katya on her stretching and warm up routine," he suggested. "Then we'll do some track work," Alex finished.

Sudha pushed herself to keep pace with all that Katya did, so much so that Alex's slight frostiness melted as he began to appreciate the virtually untutored talent of the Indian runner.

"Not bad," he complimented the two athletes at the end of the track session. "We will try a few hurdles and then we're finished here," Alex stated. "You first, Katya," he said.

Katya moved to a marker placed twenty metres from the practice hurdle. She started her run and leapt, her right foot landing on the track beyond. She continued for six paces, turned and jogged back.

"Okay," judged Alex. "Right, Sudha, off you go," Alex instructed.

Sudha copied what she had watched Katya do and jogged back to Alex for his judgement. Alex shook his head. "Look

Sudha, you're slowing down as you come to the hurdle. You must attack the barrier, not stutter into it," he said.

"But I have to get my stride right for the jump. Is that not so?" Sudha queried.

"Sure, sure you do but you must trust your eyes and your legs. Accelerate into the barrier; the adjustments will be automatic," Alex said quietly, soothing Sudha's anxiety. "Watch Katya closely," he said. "Okay, Katya," he nodded for her to start. Katya completed the run and jump. "Did you notice her acceleration?" Alex asked Sudha.

"I will try," said Sudha apprehensively. She ran at the hurdle, stretching the last stride so that her left foot landed atop the hurdle. Her right foot flew over the beam and onto the track beyond.

"How did that feel?" Alex asked.

"Better, much better," Sudha replied with relieved enthusiasm.

"Practice the approach to the hurdles, accelerate in, then drive with your right foot and accelerate away. You will see that it will save you a lot of time each lap," Alex counselled.

"Right, four more will be enough for this morning," Alex addressed Katya.

After they had completed their programme, an official arrived. "Katya Schmidt needs to go to doping control when you have finished," he said, handing Alex a chit with the request.

"I'll need some more fluid," Katya addressed Alex who tossed her a small, plastic bottle which advertised its energy-giving properties on the label. "If I don't drink, I could be waiting hours to pass a sample," Katya said to Sudha, grimacing.

Alex caught the drinks bottle as Katya flicked it back towards him.

"Tomorrow is the Opening Ceremony and I know you

would like to go, Katya. It will make it difficult to train in the morning but I actually believe that's not such a bad thing," said Alex, watching Katya's delighted smile. "As you will be racing forty eight hours later, a light gym session early on Sunday afternoon, say at three p.m., would be a good idea," he suggested.

"Sure," Katya concurred.

"It was a pleasure to meet you," Alex said, shaking Sudha's hand.

"Good luck with your qualifier on Monday and remember, attack the obstacles," he said, letting his hand slide from Sudha's fingers.

"Thank you. It's been most interesting, most enlightening," Sudha replied.

"Katya, I will go with you to doping control," Alex offered.

"Yes please," Katya replied. "See you on Monday," Katya said to Sudha.

"Most definitely," Sudha responded. "Thank you so much for sharing your training session with me."

"It was fun," Katya replied. "Thank you."

After they had visited the doping control and Katya had given her sample, Alex sat beside her on the bus to the village.

"What opinion do you have of Sudha?" Katya asked Alex.

"She has natural talent," Alex replied.

"How do you feel about your own form?" Alex enquired.

"I've never felt fitter, more in control," Katya mused. "I feel I can run faster than I have ever run before. I know it's arrogant of me to say so but I do feel invincible," she confided.

"Good, good," Alex responded, pensively.

Chapter 28

KATYA opened the door of her apartment and dropped her kitbag on the spare bed. Silke and Katryn were not there. She stripped off her damp kit, draped it across the cold radiators and showered. Dressed in a clean shirt and shorts, Katya wrote a note to her flatmates.

Gone to the team office for tickets/village passes.
Back in 30 mins.
Katya
P.S. It's now 2.15.

In the team office, Katya filled in the forms requesting passes for her parents and Anya to visit the village on Sunday. She studied the cultural events on offer and applied for tickets to a performance by the Philharmonic Orchestra from seven p.m. to nine p.m. on the Thursday evening. Anya would appreciate the concert and they could spend time together with Katya's parents, the day before the final. Perhaps they could have an early dinner before the concert, Katya considered. She handed her completed forms to the volunteer who was performing the role of an unpaid administrator. Christoph Kleim walked into the office.

"Hello Katya," he said, smiling. "How can I be of service?" he asked.

"I'm applying for visitor passes for my parents and companion and also for tickets for the concert on Thursday evening," Katya replied.

Christoph took the forms from the volunteer and signed the bottom of each in the authorisation box provided. He handed them back to the volunteer.

"Can I be of any further assistance?" Christoph offered.

"No, thank you," Katya responded.

Silke and Katryn were both in the apartment when Katya returned. "You're looking pleased with yourself, Katryn," Katya commented.

"Like the cat that drank the cream," added Silke.

"Mmmm...," Katryn responded, licking her lips, her eyelids descending over her eyes.

"Come on Katryn, tell us," Silke implored.

"Perhaps it's a secret," Katryn teased.

Changing tack, Katya said, "I'm going to the Opening Ceremony tomorrow. How about you two?"

"Yes, I want to go," Silke replied.

"The Opening Ceremony sounds like it could be fun. I'm in," Katryn said.

"I picked up this timetable at the office," Katya said, holding out a single A4 sheet. "It says we must assemble at one p.m. at muster point B."

"The Opening Ceremony doesn't start till six. Why do we have to assemble five hours earlier?" Katryn complained.

Katya shrugged. "That's what the instructions say," she replied.

"And where is muster point B," Katryn continued, aggressively.

"I don't...oh, here is a map on the back of the sheet," Katya said, turning over the document. "It's very close, less than one hundred metres from here."

"I went to the Opening Ceremony in Barcelona," Silke said. "It's really good. There's a great party atmosphere. We'll be fed and watered and have plenty of time to meet other teams," she enthused.

"A chance to mingle," said Katryn more positively.

"Yes," Silke confirmed. "You're absolutely right."

"What time are you eating tonight?" Katya asked Silke.

"About seven thirty, in the city. My parents and brother are here and they are taking me to dinner," Silke replied. "You're welcome to come too if you want to join us," Silke offered.

"No, thank you but it was really kind of you to offer," replied Katya.

"I've got a date tonight, vodka with cream," said Katryn, mysteriously.

"Ah-ha! That's why you were looking so pleased with yourself, Katryn. Who is he? Tell us more," Silke pleaded.

"I will when it's over. It's great here having the opportunity to meet so many other people. This one is really rather special so I don't want to tempt fate. I'll tell you all about it later."

Katya smiled as Silke threw a pillow at Katryn in frustration. Lying on her right side on the bed, she picked up the novel she had started reading the previous night. The book opened at page seven, the top corner of the page folded in. Fifteen minutes later, Katya folded over the top of page ten and, gripping her pillow in both arms, squashed her face into it to doze.

When she awoke, Katya was confused by her surroundings. It took a moment for her to remember where she was. The apartment was quiet. Silke and Katryn must have left, she surmised. Panic then set in. How long had she slept. The dials on her wristwatch calmed her heartbeat. It was ten past six in the evening she interpreted, time to wash and go to the dining area.

Katya loaded her tray with pasta, salad and fruit and then found an empty twelve seat table to sit at.

"Mind if I join you?" said an American accent.

"Not at all," Katya replied to the five foot nine, dark-haired, brown-eyed woman. "It must be eight years since we last met," Katya continued.

"Seoul, 1998," confirmed Shannon Whelan, now Mrs Shannon Myers. "But we didn't really get the opportunity to talk to each other then," she said.

"Perhaps if you have time, we can talk now," Katya suggested.

"Yes, I would like to," Shannon responded.

"I understand you've had a husband and children since then," Katya queried.

"Yes, Jamie Myers. I met him in Seoul. He was on the US rowing team. He medalled in the coxless fours. I can remember the first time I saw him at a reception in Seoul. He was tall, six four, had shaggy, out-of-control, blonde hair, a crooked smile, crooked teeth and blue eyes to melt ice cream. I fell in love with him that instant," Shannon gushed, brown eyes sparkling with love's dew. "We dated in Seoul and our parents met there. He came to the celebrations afterwards in my home town, Beaver Creek in Montana. There are only four hundred and fifty people living there but I swear the reception they gave us was as good as any ticker tape parade in New York. The folks were so proud that one of their own had won an Olympic silver. As I rode down Main Street on a trailer, decked out with red, white and blue and pulled by two white horses, Cinderella couldn't have felt prouder than I did that day. Jamie was beside me then, his silver medal round his neck. The folks nearly took as much pride in him as they did with me," Shannon eulogised.

Katya's memory was stirred by Shannon's description of the Beaver Creek community's applause of their heroine. She remembered her village and the walk she had made down Main Street twenty years ago, after she had won the under-thirteen Regional Championship at eight hundred metres. Her eyes clouded with salty water.

"Are you OK?" Shannon asked, noticing Katya close to tears.

"Yes, I'm fine," Katya replied. "The reception you received, the way you recall it, it's very moving," said Katya. "Please, go on," Katya asked. Shannon continued.

"That evening, we had the best hog roast in the living memory of anyone who has lived in Beaver Creek all their lives. There was feasting, music and dancing and that's when Jamie and I knew we would spend the rest of our time together. The hoopin' and a hollering when we announced our engagement was something to behold. It was only five weeks since we'd met. Beaver Creek isn't renowned for long engagements. Wedding invitations were sent out. Jamie's folks came west from Boston and we were married on Thanksgiving. Less than four months since the day I fell in love with him, my name changed from Miss Shannon Whelan to Mrs Shannon Myers."

"How many children do you have? How old are they?" Katya asked.

"Frank's our first born. His seventh birthday is on the twenty-fifth of next month. He was a big baby, ten pounds six ounces. Boy, Katya, I'll tell ya, giving birth to Frank is easily the most painful experience of my life. Running only hurts for minutes, then you're recovering. Sixteen hours I laboured giving birth to Frank but it's worth every minute of it now, now that it's over. At the time, I wanted to quit, begged, prayed, pleaded for an end . . . .," Shannon stopped. "Katya, are you sure you're OK?" Shannon asked tenderly, taking hold of Katya's left hand and compressing it between her own.

"Yes, yes," Katya replied, wiping the tears from her

cheeks with her right hand. "Does Frank have any interest in sport?" Katya asked.

"He's mad keen on soccer," Shannon responded, unsure as to Katya's well-being.

"Do they play soccer in Montana?" Katya queried, now recovered.

"Probably but we live in Connecticut now, in New England. Jamie works for a medical equipment company. Soccer has really taken off there for girls as wells as boys. Frank plays in a local league for his age group. His team has a good coach; they seem to win most of their games. Frank can run as fast as any other boy his age at school. His first sister, Annie, is five. She was born on the fifteenth of March, 1991. Eight pounds four ounces and under four hours in labour, Annie has always been easy. She's just started to learn the piano and she swims like a fish though under the water rather than on top. She pops up for a lungful of air and then she's gone under again. Folks from back home in Beaver Creek say she looks a lot like me but I see more of Jamie in her." Shannon's breast heaved contentedly at the association. She continued, "Joanne's the little one, just turned three; her birthday is the twenty-second of May. She's our Barcelona babe."

"What's the connection?" Katya asked, puzzled.

"AUGUST, ninety-two, MAY, ninety-three," Shannon emphasized the months.

"Oh, of course," Katya responded, smiling at the obviousness of the link.

"Joanne was the same weight as Annie but only two hours in coming. If we have any more I might not make it to the hospital," Shannon said, laughing.

"Will you have more?" Katya asked.

"Probably. We'll see after Friday," said Shannon smiling, the flick of her right eyelid, affirmation.

"Why do you still race?" Katya asked. "You have a wonderful husband and family. What is it that you still strive for?" she continued.

"Well, to beat you," Shannon bounced back her reply. "But, aside from beating you," Shannon said, considering her answer, "I've thought about it quite a bit, discussed it many times with Jamie. He stopped top level rowing after Seoul. The most common conclusion is that I'm afraid to retire. I've been racing for twenty years, won national championships, world titles, Olympic medals, silver in Seoul, Gold in Barcelona. Not training, not racing is an issue I have to confront one day but deep, deep inside, I still feel I have something to prove to myself," Shannon looked into Katya's eyes as she concluded.

"Me too, I feel I still have something to prove to myself, just to myself," Katya responded, emphasising her last words and holding Shannon's gaze.

"Hey, enough of me. Tell me of your triumphs and failures since Seoul," Shannon asked. "Do you have a husband? Do you have kids?" Shannon added.

"No husband, no children, many failures, a few triumphs. It is a long, sad story. Are you certain you want to hear?" Katya enquired.

"Hey, I'm really interested. I'm not rushing anywhere. It's eight years since we last met. You dropped from the athletics' radar for six of them. Sure, I want to hear your story," Shannon said emphatically.

Katya inhaled, "On the man issue, I formed a physical relationship with my coach, Dieter Muller. We slept together and by February of 1988, my pregnancy was confirmed. Dieter asked me to keep training. He continued to give me pink and blue vitamin tablets, watching over me to make sure I swallowed them. My training times improved. In March, my times were faster than ever before but I

165

continued to ask Dieter why, why was I training? I would be eight months into my pregnancy by the scheduled first race in Seoul. He said it was important because my performances were a motivational benefit to the other athletes. Late in May, I was called to the clinic and received an injection. This was not an unusual procedure but my reaction that evening was not normal. I started to get stomach pains. Then they became more intense. Dieter took me back to the clinic. At ten p.m., I was no longer pregnant. Dieter consoled me, told me that there was a problem with the foetus. He said it was for the best that they had to abort the foetus to protect my health. He always said foetus. He never once called it a baby. They wouldn't tell me if it was a girl or a boy. Within three days, I was training again, still taking my vitamin pills until a few weeks before we left for Seoul. As you saw, we were kept apart from the athletes of other nations, always chaperoned in Seoul. The racing you know about, the result, a further gold star on the international prestige card of the D.D.R.," Katya hesitated, "Shannon, the gold medal given to me in Seoul is a source of great shame. I know I did not beat you fairly, sportingly. It is important to me that you understand. I do not believe, no true sportswoman can ever believe, that the end justifies the means. For me, the ethos of sport, its purpose defines that to cheat is to lose. Please accept that this is my sporting faith," Katya's eyes implored acceptance.

Shannon looked into Katya's eyes, beyond, into her soul. "Katya, I do accept that you did not win in Seoul. I do believe what you say but I also did not win in Seoul," Shannon replied resolutely.

"There is nothing I can do to change Seoul," said Katya, shaking her head.

"What you have just said helps a lot, Katya," Shannon responded. "I had no notion that you had been pregnant that year. I'm truly sorry," Shannon consoled. "Would you like a cup of coffee?" asked Shannon, rising from the table.

"Yes, please, black," Katya replied.

Shannon returned with two cups of coffee. "Thank you," said Katya as Shannon placed one cup in front of her and kissed Katya on her left cheek.

"What happened after Seoul?" Shannon asked.

"I became pregnant again. Dieter felt in some way to blame for the death of our first baby. After four months, he left me. The old D.D.R. was disintegrating and suddenly there was no money, no apartment. I should have gone home to my village, to my mother and father. I didn't. The village is a little old-fashioned. I didn't have a husband. I was living in a hostel, working in a hotel as a chambermaid six months into the pregnancy, tiny feet tickling the inside of my tummy. I was cleaning a toilet in a room one Friday when I felt dampness on the inside of my thigh. I stood up and blood was trickling down my leg. I was taken to hospital. They couldn't stop the bleeding. My daughter was born lifeless. I could have joined her, often wished I had. We could have gone to God together and then at least, I would have known her. They . . . ," Katya stopped, unable to talk through the ache in her throat. Tears washed her face, soaking the top of her t-shirt. Shannon moved quickly, held her rival in her arms, clasped her to her breast as the emotion pouring from Katya's eyes juddered her upper body. Shannon released Katya when the sobbing subsided. "I did warn you it was a long, sad, story." Katya looked down at her hands lying in her lap and, sighing deeply, calmed her emotions. She looked up and smiled at Shannon bravely, "They transfused me, replacing the blood I was losing," she said.

"Are you sure you want to continue?" Shannon asked.

"Yes," Katya replied. "They removed my womb to stop the bleeding but I didn't know this at the time. It was some days later they told me," Katya swallowed to hold her tears but Shannon, beside her, was less successful as tears rolled from her glistening, brown eyes. Katya continued, "When I left the hospital, I was empty, completely empty. I wanted nothing. I needed no one. I slept in doorways, under bridges, in the park. I ate hardly at all but I didn't die. I had no chance to meet my daughter. Then, one day, I did meet her after drinking a bottle of spirits I found next to a dead man. I took it from his hand. It had worked for him so maybe it would work for me. It did. I met my daughter somehow and she was seven years old. We played. We ran through pastures of mountain flowers. She was so beautiful, so innocent but I awoke. From then on I searched for bottles of spirits, the key to unlock my imagination's door. I drank but the images of my daughter became fuzzier. Dark creatures invaded our world. One morning I awoke but I was not awake. I saw the eye of the monster as it moved to consume me, then nothing. I regained consciousness in a hospital bed, my body clean, washed for the first time in two years. One of the nurses who tended me, recognised me. She was my present coach's sister. Alex had trained me ten years earlier until he suddenly disappeared and was replaced by Dieter.

"Yes, I'm sure I met him then," Shannon interjected.

Katya continued, "Two days later, my father and mother appeared in the doorway of the hospital room. That was the most joyous moment in my life. There were enough tears to drown all three of us," Katya exaggerated. "They had visited Dresden many times searching for me, questioning people, showing my photograph. They had posters printed. They had visited the police stations, the hospitals and now they had found me, they took me back home, back to our chalet in the mountains. Adie, my woollen lamb, rested on my pillow in my bedroom. At home, I could feel myself healing. We walked in the mountains and then, one day, we walked to the village. The people we saw seemed genuinely pleased to see me. Everything was so familiar. On the way back from the village, I asked my mother if she would like a cup of coffee. She told me she would so I ran ahead to put the kettle on. As I did, the breeze whispered on my face and I lengthened my stride, running, running again, feeling the power in my legs. That evening, I decided I wanted to run, to race again," said Katya.

"When did Alex start coaching you?" Shannon asked.

"About six months after I decided to race again. Until then, I ran in the mountains. My father, Paul, was a champion runner. He coached me until I went to the Institute. He started to help me again. My mother, Heidi, is a champion cook and from her table I recovered my lost weight," Katya said, patting her tummy.

"No man in your life?" Shannon asked.

"Paul, my father," Katya replied. "There is no man in my life now but I've met a special person who is my emotional partner. Her name is Anya. She's a musician. We're not in love but we do enjoy each other's company. We've lived together for almost two years now and hopefully we will stay together forever," Katya said. "So, that's my story. I've come back to the Olympics to answer a question," Katya concluded.

"Wow, Katya, that's some life. It's been great to meet you again and, whatever happens on Friday, I hope we can stay in touch," Shannon said, rising to her feet, thoughtfully.

"I hope you have the best race you've ever run," Katya responded sincerely, shaking Shannon's hand. Shannon pulled Katya towards her in a bear hug and, as she walked away, turned to Katya, a warm smile spreading across her face. Katya returned the smile and watched Shannon leave. Exhausted, she returned to the apartment. Katryn and Silke had not returned. Katya lay on her bed, opened her book at page ten, closed it again and slept for twelve hours.

Chapter 29

SATURDAY

KATRYN and Silke were just going out through the doorway of the apartment when Katya woke.

"Good morning, Katya," Silke said. "You've slept well."

"What time is it?" Katya asked.

"Five past nine... a.m. that is. You haven't missed the Opening Ceremony," Katryn replied, glancing at her wristwatch. "We're going for breakfast. You can meet us there," Katryn added before Silke had a chance to offer to wait.

Silke and Katryn had finished their meals when Katya found the table that they were seated at.

"How was the meal with your parents?" Katya asked Silke.

"The food was ordinary but it was great to see my parents and Joachim, my little brother."

"How old is Joachim?" Katryn asked.

"He's twenty," Silke replied.

"How tall?" Katryn enquired.

"Six foot two," Silke responded.

"Well, he doesn't sound very little to me," Katryn concluded.

"He's younger than me so he will always be my LITTLE brother," Silke replied, crossly.

"And how was your evening, Katryn?" Katya asked.

"Disappointing. My date is competing on Monday and wanted to be in bed early."

"That's not normally disappointing for you," Silke rejoined.

"On his own, nitwit," Katryn retorted. "Come on, we've three hours and one bathroom to become glamorous for the television cameras at the Opening Ceremony," Katryn continued. "I'll shower and dry my hair first," she offered, pushing back her chair and leaving.

"What did you do yesterday evening?" Silke asked Katya.

"It was very interesting. I met Shannon Myers, my main rival...," Katya said as Silke interjected.

"The current Olympic champion in your event? What did you talk about?"

"Mostly about the past. She's married and has three children," Katya said. "Come on, let's go and get ready."

Katryn was using the shower when they returned to the apartment. "You go next," Silke suggested to Katya.

"I will braid your hair for you. It would look really pretty," Silke offered.

"No thanks. I think I'd prefer to keep it straight," Katya replied.

By one p.m., Katya, Silke and Katryn did look glamorous in their team uniforms.

"Carry the hats. Don't wear them," Silke advised. "They hide your face and destroy your hair," Silke's counselling continued.

Five hours and a year's excitement later, they heard the Opening Ceremony begin. All teams now assembled in echelon, Greece first, then alphabetical order until the host country, the USA, entered last. Ten minutes after the Ceremony began, the Greek flag bearer entered the stadium. The parade of athletes had started. Television cameras appeared from every angle, on hoists, on fixed platforms but mostly hand-held, assistants feeding out umbilical cords behind the crouching, backward-crabbing cameramen. Twenty minutes after Greece entered, the German team had advanced to the tunnel leading into the stadium. They had passed through the canyon of well-wishers, through the corridor of security personnel and now they could see part of the crowd they had been listening to, cheering each nation on as they entered the stadium. Silke, Katryn and Katya marched, one behind the other, each on the outside of their line as Silke had instructed them to do in the knowledge that that would be the area covered best by television shots.

Katya's tummy tingled. "Germany," boomed the announcer as they marched into the lights. The applause swelled as their team name was called. Silke was right, television cameramen scurried backwards, pointing their cameras at the smiling, cheering faces of the athletes on the outside of each line.

Katya's ambitions evaporated the moment she stepped into the stadium. All thoughts of personal success were swamped by the celebration she was a part of. Her spirit lifted in a manner she could not recollect. She looked into the crowd but identifying her parents and Anya in the many hued mosaic of smiling eyes was beyond Katya's powers of recognition as she walked, waving to the crowds, waving to the Presidents.

Now seated, Katya applauded the other teams still entering the stadium. Eventually, the mightiest roar bounced off the eardrums of the crowd as the host nation, the United States of America, was introduced.

The arrival of the Olympic flame, the address by the President of the International Olympic Committee, the acceptance by the chairman of the Atlanta Organising Committee and the opening by the President of the United States of America were a blur. For Katya, the most spiritual moments were the entry of the Olympic flag and the Athletes' Oath. As she gazed at the Olympic flame, now lit atop the stadium, she felt the same comfort of community that she remembered from her childhood. She was among people who shared common ideals. She was at one with them. She was an Olympian.

Turning to Silke, Katya said, "Do you feel special to be a part of this?"

"Yes, I do," Silke replied, hugging her team-mate and kissing her cheek.

The final act of the spectacular show left the arena. Katya and Silke made their way to the exit amongst the throng of athletes. Katryn had set off to mingle! They arrived back at the village after eleven p.m. and were among the first in the dining area fortunately as the whole of the athlete population sought to eat at the same time. Katya and Silke ate quickly, yielding their seats to two Australian men standing beside their table.

At the apartment, Katya was in bed within a few minutes and asleep shortly afterwards. Silke kissed Katya's sleeping head and, pulling back the sheet and blanket, climbed into her own bed.

Chapter 30

SUNDAY

KATYA awoke. She stretched, pressing her fingertips against the headboard and pointing her toes at the opposite wall. She turned to the travel clock on her bedside table; twenty minutes past seven was the comforting recognition. Katya dreamily allowed herself forty minutes of waking sleep to indulge in before she would slide from her nest. She pushed the side of her pillow further under her and then squashed it between her encircling arms. Her mama and papa were coming to see her today. It was June when she had last seen them, almost two months. Anya would be with them. Katya chuckled at the prospect. The conversation would be a spit-roast of words as each jostled to impart their news, eager to be polite, bursting to talk.

Katya's eyes peered from under her lids at her travel clock; seven dot three two, the red numbers, set in the black face, told her; not time to get up yet, Katya relished, closing her eyes and squeezing the pillow.

"Are you awaa . . . kke?" Silke asked, mid-yawn.

Katya opened her eyes and rolled over to face Silke's bed. "I am now," she replied, softening the last word as she realised that Katryn was asleep in the bed below.

Silke picked up on the nuance and whispered loudly, "What are your plans for today?"

"My parents and my friend, Anya, are coming to the

village. Then I have a gym session at three. What are you going to do?" Katya replied.

"I'm going to the track this morning. I have a session with my coach, Jurgen, at ten, then a gym session this afternoon. Perhaps we could go to the gym together?" Silke queried.

Katryn moaned, rolled over in her bed, knocking her duvet partly to the floor. The rest of the duvet followed slowly, sliding from Katryn's naked body.

"Mmm," Silke exhaled, arching eyebrows as she lent over her bunk to gaze on Katryn's naked back and buttocks below.

"We don't want to wake her. Let's decide over breakfast," Katya replied, stretching her arms upwards as she stood beside her bed. "You can use the bathroom first," she continued, picking up Katryn's fallen duvet and placing it over her sleeping teammate.

After breakfast, Katya went to the visitors' reception lounge. As she sat waiting for her parents and Anya, she smiled, observing the reunion of other athletes and their families. Airport-tears of happiness flowed as they crunched each other in bear hugs. Teenage brothers and sisters looked uncomfortable with the un-cool emotions shown by their younger and older relatives. Katya witnessed the reunion of lovers, aware only of each other, faces, lips pressed together as if the last moments of the world were now. She witnessed the meeting of athletes and their sponsors, the latter as much interested in the surroundings as the athletes.

Anxiety tightened Katya's chest. Had she told her parents and Anya to bring their passports? They would need to exchange them as security for their visitors' passes. Then, just as she remembered she had, allaying her fears, Paul, Heidi and Anya appeared. Their passes, hung on ribbons round their necks, clashed with Katya's pass as they embraced in reunion.

Katya led her guests through the village. "It's a university campus, so big that it has its own internal bus system," she said as a bus passed them. "You can tell which teams are accommodated in each building by the national flags the athletes have draped out of the windows. This is our building. I will show you the rooms I share. Then we'll have lunch."

Katya knocked on her door, then opened it and looked in. Silke had left but Katryn was still asleep, her duvet on the floor again. Katya blocked the entrance. "Wait here a moment," she said, turning to her visitors. Katya entered, closing the door behind her and, once again, placed the fallen duvet on Katryn's naked body, tucking it in under her to stop it sliding off.

Katryn awoke, "What's happening?" she asked.

"Its eleven thirty and I am showing my parents the village. They are outside the door now, waiting to come in," Katya said.

"Oh shit," Katryn replied, wrapping herself in the duvet. "I'm decent now so you can show them in."

After a swift tour of their apartment, Katya arrived at the dining hall. She handed in the meal tickets she had purchased for her guests. A few minutes later, they placed their laden trays on a twelve seat table occupied by three Egyptian and two French athletes.

"Well, I've been waiting to tell you but I didn't want to interrupt your tour," Heidi began.

"How's training?" Paul took advantage of Heidi's pause to ask.

"Fine . . . ," Katya replied.

"You're looking great," Anya complimented.

"Well, as I was saying," Heidi continued, "The local paper has a three page article about you, very complimentary, as it should be," Heidi affirmed.

177

Katya, Paul and Anya ate as Heidi recounted the merits of the article, the gossip from the village and a new diet she had discovered. Paul finished eating and admonished Heidi.

"Heidi, we've all finished and you haven't even started yet," he said.

"Oh, sorry. I'll hurry. It's only salad. That's all that's on my diet for lunch," Heidi retorted, slicing her knife through cold cuts of turkey, beef and ham.

"What are your tactics for the heat tomorrow?" Paul asked, having turned Heidi's attention to her plate.

"I'll discuss them with Alex this afternoon but I expect the pace to be quite slow. Then I'll rehearse my last six hundred metres, running as fast as I am able. This is my only chance to do this as the semi-final will be much more competitive. What do you think?" Katya enquired.

"Your serious competitors will then be aware of your finishing burst but it's important for you to know, so, on balance, it's a good plan," Paul concluded.

"I've booked tickets for all of us for a performance by the Philharmonic Orchestra this Thursday. Perhaps we could eat first at a restaurant close by," Katya said.

"But your final's on Friday," said Paul, anxiously.

"Yes but the concert finishes at 9.00 p.m. so I should be in bed by 10.00 p.m. which is ideal," Katya replied.

"I would really like to go but only if it doesn't affect your racing," Anya said.

"No, it will be a good preparation to keep me calm," Katya responded.

"It will be good to see you, to wish you all the best, one last hug," Heidi said, having consumed her salad.

"You've got a training session this afternoon. It's best we let you get ready," said Paul, rising from the table, tray in hand.

On the walk back to the visitor reception lounge, they

passed a large section of scaffolding on the perimeter of the village.

"What's that for, over there?" Heidi enquired.

"It's the temporary grandstand for the swimming events," Katya replied. "Fortunately, we are well away from the noise."

At the visitors' centre, Heidi and Paul hugged and kissed their only daughter. Anya and Katya hugged gently.

"See you on Thursday," said Katya as they passed through the exit doorway. "I'll book a restaurant and let you know the time and place."

"Italian's best... plenty of pasta," Paul said as he waved goodbye.

Katya returned to her room to change for her gym session. Silke was waiting for her. Katryn was at the track, training. "Did your parents enjoy the tour?" Silke asked.

"Yes, except for a nearly embarrassing moment with Katryn. She was still in bed when they came," Katya replied.

"She told me. She liked your Dad," Silke responded. "What about your friend? Was she pleased to see you?" Silke continued.

"Anya... yes, we were happy to see each other," Katya answered, picking up the smaller of her two kitbags. "I'm ready," she concluded.

After the gym session, Katya sipped from a bottle of mineral water. Alex drank black, unsweetened coffee from his cup. They sat in the athletes' lounge, discussing the race plan for Monday's heats. At four fifteen in the afternoon, the lounge was unusually quiet.

"What's the weather forecast for tomorrow morning?" Katya enquired.

"Twenty eight degrees, no rain, lowish humidity," Alex replied. "Your heat is due to start at 11.10 which is close to

179

the time that Friday's final will be run," he continued. "This is a useful rehearsal opportunity."

"I plan to be in bed by ten. I'd rather be really tired and sleep quickly than go to bed at nine and not sleep. I will set my alarm for six which shouldn't be too much of a problem for Silke and Katryn as they are not competing tomorrow; they can roll over and go back to sleep. Then we can meet here for breakfast at seven," Katya said, looking at Alex for his approval.

"Sounds good," Alex responded. "We should get a bus for the stadium at about eight which leaves us plenty of leeway if there are any transport glitches. What are your thoughts on the race?" he asked.

"Well, it will probably be run quite slowly as six of the ten runners qualify for the semis. The seeding means that many of my main rivals are in the other three heats. If it is run at a slow pace, I can practice my finish from six hundred metres out and then give my all in the last two hundred," Katya replied.

"Even if the pace is faster than you hope, it may be useful to quicken with six hundred to go," Alex responded. "Accelerate in and clear the hurdle five hundred out, just as we have been practising. This should give you two to three metres' advantage if any other runner is trying to stay with you," he concluded.

"Right, that's what I'll do then," affirmed Katya.

Alex stood up, the empty, plastic, coffee cup in his right hand. Katya walked with him to the exit, placing their empty bottle and cup in the waste bins on the way out.

"What are you going to do now?" Alex asked.

"I want to check my e-mails, then send a few. I'm meeting Silke and Katryn at six for dinner," Katya replied.

"Okay, I'll see you for breakfast at seven tomorrow morning," Alex said as he left.

Katya got up to date with her e-mails. She had dinner with her teammates, read three chapters of a novel by Fleck and was asleep by ten.

Chapter 31

MONDAY

ALEX and Katya arrived at the stadium at eight forty. Three hours later, they left. Katya had run her race as they had planned. Her winning margin of thirty metres had been achieved with easy effort. All her main rivals also qualified easily but seventeen of the forty-one entrants were eliminated. Sudha Lall had beaten her pessimistic forecast and would run in the semi-finals on Wednesday.

On the bus back to the village, Alex and Katya discussed the other heats as well as Katya's race.

"Do you need a massage?" Alex asked in a tone which indicated that he thought it would be beneficial.

"I don't feel at all tight," Katya replied, bending and kneading the underside of her thigh and calf muscles with her fingertips. "Maybe I'll go over to physio after lunch. It can't do any harm and it may help," she said, sitting upright again.

"There is a team captains' meeting in the village this afternoon. The draw for the semi-finals should be available at about four p.m.," Alex said.

"I'll be out, I'm afraid," Katya replied. "I'm booked to go to a local junior school who have adopted Germany for the duration of the Games," she continued.

"That's not a problem. I'll leave a copy of the draw under your door," Alex responded.

"We're here," said Katya as the bus stopped, brakes hissing, the automatic doors folding open. "Shall we go straight to lunch? I am very hungry," said Katya.

"I notice you didn't have much of an appetite at breakfast," Alex retorted.

"What's new?" giggled Katya, famous for her low appetite before a race.

Little was said over lunch as Katya re-fuelled her body. "That was impressive," Alex commented when Katya's plates were bare. "You probably need at least an hour's rest before you go to the physio," he concluded.

"Well it's ten past one now," said Katya, turning her wrist to view her watch face. "If I see the physio at two thirty for half an hour, I should be ready to leave for the school at three thirty," Katya calculated. "What's tomorrow's programme?" she asked.

"Go for a forty minute jog around the village tomorrow morning and then I'll meet you in the gym at three p.m. for a light session," Alex instructed.

"Okay, see you at three," Katya replied, rising from the table to return to her flat.

"Well done," Katryn leapt up and kissed Katya's cheek as she walked into the apartment. "I watched your race on television. That was some jump over the fixed hurdle on the penultimate lap and I know because I'm a jumper," Katryn continued, squishing Katya in an enthusiastic embrace.

"Thank you," Katya replied as the air was squeezed from her lungs and her lunch almost followed. "I need to lie down now. I've eaten for two and I've booked a massage in just over an hour," Katya said as Katryn disentangled her encircling arms.

"Right, well, I am off to lunch now so I will leave you in tranquillity. I think that's the appropriate word," laughed Katryn as she bounced out of the door.

183

Katya plopped down on her bed, satisfied with her first race. I need to feel as content after each of my next two races she told herself. Then, contradicting this notion, she decided that as long as she qualified from the semi-final, it did not have to be a good race. In the final, however, she needed to be satisfied with her performance. Katya drifted into tranquillity. She awoke suddenly, her body flinching at an anticipated fall. Having regained full consciousness, she glanced at the digital clock on the bedside cabinet. 14.15, the red numbers told her. She had fifteen minutes to make her physio appointment.

By three twenty five, Katya, in her team blazer and skirt, stood with six other athletes from the German team, waiting at the kerbside. A minibus pulled alongside the group and Christoph Kleim counted them into their seats before seating himself next to the driver. As the bus left the Olympic Village through the twelve feet high, double, security gates, he turned to address Katya in the row of seats behind.

"You ran well today. How are you feeling?"

"Thank you. I've just had a thirty minute massage. The physio certainly worked the lactic acid from my legs."

"Good, good. It will take us about fifty minutes to get to the school," he said, addressing all of the athletes. "I have made these goodwill visits at previous Olympics and they are always very much appreciated by the local communities," he concluded, turning to face the road ahead. Katya dozed, her head on the side window gently vibrating with the motion of the bus.

They arrived at the Decatur High School five minutes early and were met by the principal, Mrs McMurty and the physical education instructor, Jane Salmon.

Mrs McMurty chatted with Christoph Kleim as she led his team's representatives to the school sports hall. Nine seats were set in a row on a dais at the end of the hall. Mrs McMurty positioned herself in the middle of the row, in front of a lectern which had a cordless microphone placed upon it. Jane Salmon arranged the German team along the seats behind. Katya sat in the last seat to the right of Mrs McMurty, smiling at the three hundred or so students in front of her.

"It is a privilege and an honour to welcome these Olympic athletes, representing Germany," Mrs McMurty said into the microphone which she had picked up from the lectern in front of her. "I would like to introduce the German Chef de Mission, Mr Christoph Kleim," she turned to Christoph who stood up, half bowed from the waist in acknowledgement and moved beside her as the students applauded. "Herr Kleim will introduce his athletes and then they will take questions," she concluded, handing the microphone to Christoph.

Christoph introduced each athlete with complimentary allusions to their prowess and humorous insights into their personal foibles. The questions followed with Christoph assuming the roll of moderator. After twenty questions had been answered and thirty to forty arms were being raised, Mrs McMurty intervened. "Two more questions only," she intoned. "We need to leave some time for those of you who would like autographs." Christoph nodded approval and chose the last two questioners.

The queue for autographs snaked around the hall and out into the corridors. After ten minutes with little noticeable change in its length, Christoph asked the echelon of six athletes on the dais to disperse, one to go to each corner of the hall and one either side at the midway doors. The queue now split six ways and each student was able to meet at least one athlete.

The minibus left the school at seven to the cheers and

applause of the students and faculty. Katya was back in the Olympic Village, having dinner, by eight. After dinner, she checked her emails. The flood from well-wishers, two hundred and eighty-three unread messages, overwhelmed her. She scanned the red listing and replied to the messages from her parents and Anya. As she pressed the send key, a firm hand gripped her left shoulder from behind.

"Hi, where have you been?" enquired Silke, kissing her on the cheek.

"Oh hi, I've been to visit a school," replied Katya, rising from her seat in front of the terminal and pressing the key to close her email address. "I'm going back to our rooms now. Where are you heading?" she asked Silke.

"Same place. I'll walk with you."

"What have you been doing today?"

"Some light road work, nothing too strenuous. I just need to stay loose for Wednesday's heat," Silke said.

"Are you feeling confident?" Katya asked.

"I'm confident I can run fast enough to make the final but, after that, well, I'll know by this time on Saturday," Silke replied.

"I won't have to wait that long. I should know my fate by midday on Friday," Katya said, "That is providing I don't mess up in Wednesday's semi final."

"You won't and you'll win on Friday," said Silke, throwing her right arm across Katya's shoulders and squeezing her right biceps between her fingers as they arrived at the door of their apartment. Katya picked up the sheet of paper on the floor as they entered. It was the draw for the semi-final. She glanced at the listings. She would race in the first semi, Shannon Myers would race in the second.

Chapter 32

TUESDAY

KATYA was woken by the vibrating alarm in her wristwatch. 06.00 a.m., it read. She pressed the alarm-off button and rose quietly from her bed to use the bathroom. She took care to avoid disturbing the sleeping Katryn and Silke.

Now washed and dressed in her training top and shorts, she quietly closed the apartment door behind her. The village streets were already peopled with athletes and trainers either leaving for their event venues or going to the dining halls for breakfast.

Katya changed her pace from a walk into a trot as she reached the road. She jogged along the roadways, nodding her head and returning nods of acknowledgement to runners passing in the opposite direction. After forty minutes, she was back at her apartment door, breathing easily, a slight moisture on her forehead the only sign of her exertions. Katryn was asleep when she entered. Silke's bed was empty. A note on Katya's bed explained, I HAVE GONE FOR A JOG. BACK AT 07.15. Katya looked at her watch. It was five past seven. She stripped off her training kit and stepped under the shower. The initial cold shock when she opened the faucet was soon replaced by the soothing balm of rods of hot water beating a tattoo on her shoulder blades. She stood, languishing in the warmth of the water until her reverie was rudely interrupted by Silke banging on the bathroom door,

"Hurry Katya, I'm horribly hot and sweaty and need to have a shower before breakfast."

Katya reluctantly turned the taps and, wrapping a towel around her, exited the bathroom. Silke darted into the bathroom complaining. "You, know, they are providing cold showers for the horses at the equestrian venue; they should do the same for us!" Katya laughed at Silke's dudgeon and then bumped into a very sleepy Katryn.

"Morning," Katryn yawned as Katya patted her body through the towel to dry herself.

"Good morning," Katya replied. "Are you coming to breakfast?"

"How long have I got to get ready?"

"Silke's using the bathroom right now. Say fifteen to twenty minutes," Katya replied, drying her back in a sawing motion with the towel held behind, one end in each hand.

Thirty minutes later, the three teammates were breakfasting together in the main dining hall, discussing their plans for the day.

"I've got a gym session at two thirty this afternoon but I'm free this morning," said Katryn.

"I'm due in the gym at three and I have completed the jog which was this morning's work," Katya added.

"I've already run this morning too so that's settled then," concluded Silke. "We can go and watch some of the other events this morning. Any ideas?"

"I read that there's an American trying for his sixth gold medal in the pool this morning," Katya said.

"Those tight swimsuits really show what a man has," said Katryn, warming to the suggestion.

"The pool is very convenient, right next to us but I bet it'll be difficult to get tickets this late," Silke counselled.

"Well, let's try," said Katya, rising from the table. "We'll go and see Christoph Kleim and ask. Nothing ventured ..."

Christoph was in the team office when they arrived at nine. "Any chance of three athletes' tickets for this morning's swimming?" Katya asked.

"Normally none," Christoph replied, "But fifty sponsors' tickets have just been released as they will not be using them. Hurry and fill in the forms and I will get you your tickets within an hour. They will be very good seats. Come back before ten."

"Yesss," whooped Katryn as they left the office having completed the necessary written requests.

At eleven thirty, the three girls watched the final of the two hundred metres backstroke from the best seats in the swimming stadium. The American failed to win his sixth gold, being beaten into second place by a teammate.

"Wow, that was some race," Silke stated.

"Yes. Did you see the Swedish swimmer in lane eight?" Katryn enquired.

"No, he didn't win a medal did he?" Silke replied.

"He didn't win a medal; he placed eighth but did you SEE HIM?" Katryn exclaimed.

"The best swimmers and the best gymnasts always seem to win multiple medals. Why do you think that is?" enquired Katya.

"It sometimes happens in athletics too," Silke said. "Sprinters can win in the 100m, 200m, 100m relay and long jump like Jesse Owens in 1936 or Carl Lewis in 1984."

"Yes, but very rarely," Katya pressed. "Swimmers and gymnasts seem to do it in every Olympics."

"Do we want to stay for the last event before lunch or shall we try to beat the crush?" asked Katryn.

"What event is it?" Katya responded.

"The women's 100m breaststroke semi-finals," Katryn replied.

"I'm with you. Let's beat the crush," said Katya.

"I think I'll stay. See you later," said Silke, rising to let the others pass to the stairway.

Katya met Alex at the gym just before three. "How do you feel now?" Alex asked at the conclusion of the session.

"Ready to race," Katya grinned.

"Let's get some fluid into you. We can discuss tomorrow's race tactics then."

In the athletes' lounge, beside the gym, they found two seats in a corner. They chose the free cold drinks from the vending machine, all Coca-Cola brands as they had exclusive rights within all Olympic venues as a Games' sponsor.

"How would you like to run your race?" Alex asked.

"Even paced, expending as little effort as possible before Friday's final," replied Katya.

"Do you want to win your semi-final?" Alex queried.

"Not particularly. Top three would be fine. Six qualify so I don't want to be caught out in a stampede for the last few places," said Katya.

"You'll need pace throughout the race to drop most of the other runners. Donat of Romania will stay with you as will Keino of Kenya probably," said Alex.

"I have to get them to share the pacemaking with me," said Katya.

"It's in their interest to, especially to avoid being caught out in a slow-run race. I'll talk to the Romanian trainer," Alex continued. "We should meet for breakfast as a rehearsal for Friday's final. I think it best we leave straight after your race tomorrow and come back to the village for lunch. We can get the result of the second semi-final when we get back. How do you feel about that?"

"Yes, that sounds like a good plan," Katya agreed.

"Oh, and the television interview, would you prefer before or after dinner?"

"After dinner," Katya said.

"Okay, I'll go and speak to Christoph now to arrange it for seven thirty tomorrow evening. I'll see you tomorrow for breakfast at seven," Alex said as he picked up his empty drink can and lobbed it into a waste bin, ten feet away. He smiled self-consciously at Katya as the can bounced from the rim into the bin. Katya followed Alex from the lounge, dropping her empty drinks bottle into the bin as she passed.

Alone at the apartment, Katya took off her damp training kit. She took the morning's running kit from the radiator and put her damp clothes in their place, alongside Katryn and Silke's drying shorts and t-shirts. After showering, she dressed in a clean, white t-shirt with a Tigger screen-print on the front, complimented by black tracksuit bottoms. Katya folded her dry kit from the radiator and placed it in the wardrobe space allocated to her. She looked at her wristwatch. "Five twenty," she mouthed as she flopped onto her bed and stretched along its length. Almost immediately, her eyelashes met.

Soft fingers on her shoulder interrupted Katya's subconscious replay of tomorrow's semi-final.

"Are you coming to dinner?" Katryn asked as Katya's eyelashes drifted apart.

"Sure. What time is it?" she asked rhetorically, glancing at her own wrist.

"Six fifteen," Katryn answered.

"Okay," she responded, swinging her legs over the side of her bed and pushing up with the palms of her hands. "We'll leave a note for Silke," she said, pushing the inside of her big toe against the leather thong of her flip-flop.

The main dining hall was crowded. Katya and Katryn, carrying their laden food trays, wandered amongst the tables, looking for two, adjoining, free spaces. A group of Japanese athletes moved their kitbags which were occupying two seats.

"Thank you," the two girls said together as they placed their trays on the table.

"The food is superb," Katryn said, scooping another spoon of soup towards her mouth. "The men too," she said, wistfully.

"You do seem to be enjoying the men," said Katya.

"SEEM... hmm that's a good word. It's just an act," replied Katryn.

"How so?" Katya asked.

Katryn's eyes brimmed with tears. "I'm still in love with someone back home. He left me two months ago after four years together... It hurts... It hurts so much... I try to distract myself," she said as the tears spilled from her eyes.

"Do you want to talk about it?" Katya asked, holding Katryn's left hand between the palms of her own.

"Not really... but thanks for the offer," Katryn said, squeezing Katya's hand. "I didn't mean to talk about him."

The Japanese athletes had left. "What sport do you think those athletes are taking part in?" Katryn asked, changing the subject and withdrawing her hand.

"They are small, good power-to-weight ratios. They're probably not boxers, maybe gymnasts," Katya surmised.

"And these?" Katryn nodded in the direction of the Greek athletes heading towards the spaces vacated by the Japanese.

"That's easy. Basketball," Katya replied as the six feet ten inch athletes sat at their table.

Katryn had now regained control of her emotions. "Let's go and check our emails," Katya suggested. "I need to send messages to my parents and Anya."

"Okay," Katryn replied, picking up her tray to take to the disposal point.

Chapter 33

WEDNESDAY, 2.00 P.M.

ALEX sat beside Katya on the bus for the village. Opposite sat a beaming Sudha Lall. She would race in the final on Friday alongside Katya. She had achieved more, much more than the Indian public had expected of her, more than she had hoped for herself. As Alex and Katya had taken their seats, each had shaken Sudha's hand and congratulated her. Seated, coach and athlete retreated to their own private world as the culmination of years of training was now focussed on the final less than forty-eight hours later.

"How are you feeling?" Alex enquired.

"Great, great," Katya replied. "Everything went as we planned. Ileana Donat helped with the early pace. Then I did my stint in front into the last lap. Joyce Keino stayed with us and, as you saw, she burst past on the finishing straight. Second place was fine for me and Ileana was happy not to race to the finish so third place was a comfortable qualifying position for her. Sudha ran brilliantly to finish fifth, don't you think?"

"Yes, I was watching you mostly but she has done well to make the final."

The bus stopped at the security checkpoint at the entrance to the village. "You go for your lunch now and I'll join you in ten minutes, once I've collected the results of the other semi-final," Alex stated as the bus entered the village.

Katya and Sudha went to the dining hall together. "I am so . . . so . . . excited," Sudha exclaimed as they sat with their food.

"Hmm I'm excited for you too . . . but now you've become a serious rival."

Sudha looked up from her salad, non-plussed at Katya's earnest demeanour. "How have I made such a change?" she asked.

"Sudha, everyone in the final is a medal contender. You improve with each race. On Friday, you will want to win; so do I."

Alex arrived with a tray in one hand and a sheet of paper in the other. "Shannon Myers won the other semi-final. Zhiming, Biwatt, Stavreva, O'Sullivan and Joseph were the other qualifiers," he said, reading from the sheet as he sat down.

"May I?" Katya asked, reaching for the result sheet. "Four seconds slower than our semi," Katya calculated.

"Yes, but we don't know what the early pace was," Alex said.

"That's true. Whatever, Friday will be tough," mused Katya.

Sudha got up to leave, "See you on Friday then," she said.

"Yes and I hope you're not waiting for me at the finish," Katya grinned.

Alex stood up and shook Sudha's hand. "Good luck," he said as Sudha left with her tray and kitbag. "Right, what's the plan for the rest of today?" Alex asked.

"I'd rather jog than do a gym session if that's alright with you?"

"Sure and you have a CBS television crew coming to interview you at 7.30, after dinner," he said.

Katya glanced at her wristwatch, "It's two forty, so, if I have a rest for a couple of hours, then jog for forty minutes, I could fit in a massage before dinner at six thirty and then the interview at seven thirty."

"Fine. We should meet tomorrow morning to discuss today's race and tactics for Friday. What time would suit you?" asked Alex.

"Say eleven. Then we can have an early lunch."

"Good. Now, don't wait for me. I'm still eating. Go and have your lie-down now," Katya rose to leave. "Oh and well done today," Alex congratulated.

Silke was leaving the apartment for her race as Katya arrived. "Well done," she said, putting her kitbag down and hugging Katya. "I watched your race on T.V."

"What time are you running?" Katya asked.

"Six ten."

"Good luck," Katya said, returning the hug.

At seven twenty five, Katya entered the interview area accompanied by Christoph Kleim. He introduced her to the CBS television reporter, Barry Petersan.

"Barry's covered a lot of Olympics. He knows the form," Christoph spoke to Katya but the message was a reminder to Barry to avoid controversy.

"We've got some good footage of your races here and some training shots. I'd like to interview you outside, talk about Friday's final and who you see as your main rivals?" said Barry.

"Sure," Katya responded.

Forty minutes later, Katya had completed her last media interview before the final.

"Thank you," she said in relief to Christoph as they left the interview area.

"You handled that well," Christoph said, extending his right hand. "Have a good race on Friday." He hesitated, "I know you have had to overcome many challenges these past eight years." Leaning forward, he kissed her on the forehead.

Katya went to the athletes' lounge to check her emails and to finalise arrangements for tomorrow's dinner and concert with Anya and her parents. Silke entered, smiling, her route to a medal still on track.

Chapter 34

THURSDAY

KATYA awoke at seven. Katryn was already dressed, Silke was awake, propped on her left elbow.

"Are you leaving now?" Katya asked Katryn.

"Yes. You two have your finals now but I must still try and qualify for mine."

"Good luck," Katya addressed Katryn as she left, her kitbag hanging from the strap on her shoulder, bouncing on her right hip.

Katya breakfasted with Silke after her jog. She met Alex, as arranged, at eleven to analyse the semi-finals and discuss tactics for the final and then, later, in the gym, for her last training session. By four forty, she was dressed for the evening. At five thirty, she was seated in an Italian restaurant with Anya and her parents.

"Have you chosen yet?" Paul asked, peering over his lowered menu at the three women.

"Anya. You choose first," Katya said.

"Veal picatta with pasta," she replied.

"That's good for me too," Katya responded.

"Heidi," Paul nodded to his wife.

"I was thinking it sounds delicious but the pasta... my diet."

"Oh I'm sure it won't hurt, just this once," Paul cajoled.

"I suppose not. Veal picatta for me too," she accepted.

Paul crooked his right index finger towards a waiter. "Yes sir. Have you chosen?"

"We'd like four veal picattas and we need to leave by six thirty," Paul said, handing the waiter his menu. "We're going to a concert."

"Anything to drink?" asked the waiter.

"Water's just fine," Paul responded, his eyes making contact with each of the women for any sign of dissent.

"Mmm... that was good," Katya said, pushing her tomato-smeared plate further towards the centre of the table.

"Six twenty," Paul read his wristwatch. "Anyone for coffee?"

"No," was the consensus reply.

Paul signalled across the restaurant for the bill by pretending to sign with an imaginary pen on an imaginary receipt. The waiter nodded his understanding and returned with the account.

They arrived at the theatre twenty minutes before the concert started. Katya was soothed by the music and the presence of the three people most precious to her. At the end of the performance, Paul hailed a taxi. "We'll ride with you to the village. Then the driver can take us to our accommodation."

The taxi ride was mostly silent. No one wanted to disturb Katya's calm.

"Thank you, thank you all for not talking about the race this evening," Katya said. "Tomorrow I will do the best I can. I am confident I will run faster than I have ever run before but this test is for me only. I need to prove something .... but only to myself."

Silence prevailed.

The taxi arrived at the security gates to the village and turned. Everyone dismounted, hugged and kissed Katya, watched her as she presented her athletes' pass and made her last wave to them as she disappeared into the village.

Chapter 35

FRIDAY

"WOMEN's three thousand metres steeplechase final," the announcer's voice boomed around the stadium. "SHANNON MYERS, United States of America." The crowd roared in support of the home country athlete as she waved tentatively, eager not to lose focus. The roll call continued, a gap between each athlete's name to allow applause. "ILEANA DONAT, Romania... JOYCE KEINO, Kenya... ROSE BIWOTT, Kenya... TERESA MARTINES, Spain... CHEN ZHIMING, People's Republic of China... SUDHA LALL, India... HEATHER O'SULLIVAN, New Zealand... KATYA SCHMIDT, Germany... ESTHER JOSEPH, Israel... YORDANKA STAVREVA, Bulgaria... KIM OK-KYUNG, Korea..."

"Take your marks," the starter ordered. Each athlete moved forward to the curved start line.

Thump... thump... thump, her heart pumping one beat per second, relaxed ready for the test, Katya, in lane three, crouched. The Romanian runner, Ileana Donat, shared the lane beside her. Right arm forward, thumb pointing up, fingers forward, left arm counterbalancing behind, Katya was ready for the start. The arc of the start line complete, twelve athletes, years of effort behind, minutes of fulfilment in front, waited. BANG. Katya leapt forward, driving her spiked soles into the rubberised track and intent on avoiding jostling elbows and the risk of stumbling in the initial scramble for position. She felt the foot of Ileana beside her, glancing off the side of her heel and then sensed her fall. Katya, raising the cadence of her legs, was free of the crush behind. Lengthening her stride and reducing the number of footfalls, Katya set her pace to test the physical and mental power of her opponents. At the first hurdle, Katya sprang, her right foot leading, then making solid contact with the track beyond. Two more hurdles were cleared. Then on she ran towards the water jump, over, SPLASH, out, wetting only one foot. Katya sailed round the bend into the home straight for the second time, over the last hurdle and past the finish line. With six laps to run, breathing easily and leading the race, Katya was elated and wanted to push harder, run faster. She remembered Alex's words, "The last two hundred metres, that is where you will win. Keep all you can for then."

Katya eased her pace till she could feel the presence of other runners behind, then settled at a speed which kept her in the lead. Joyce Keino of Kenya burst past twenty metres before the water jump. Katya, surprised, stumbled at the jump, both feet landing in the water. Chen Zhiming of China passed her on the inside. Ileana Donat of Romania, recovered from her early fall, had caught the other runners and passed Katya on the outside to move into third place behind Zhiming and Keino.

Katya was now running in fourth place. Down the finishing straight, she looked up at the giant screen to her right. Shannon Myers was a few paces behind her. She was likely to be her strongest challenger. Keino was now ten metres in front. Katya questioned her pace. Should she respond and quicken to catch the African? Her instinct answered in the negative. The danger would come from the American. She increased her pace, as did the athletes immediately around her. Keino's burst of speed seemed to be faltering and the group closed. With two laps to the finish, Katya anticipated the pain, was alert to it and pushed through it to taste the higher level of intense suffering that defines the champions from the best. Katya moved into the lead. The first hurdle on the penultimate lap was five metres in front. Katya, fatigued, checked her stride to ensure she could jump the hurdle, arching her right leg forward. She sensed a runner beside her. Shannon Myers leapt the hurdle without breaking stride. Katya was now behind. The manner in which Shannon passed her in the air stunned her. Shannon has enough left in her legs to clear the solid hurdle, no fear of clipping the top and falling, she thought.

Shannon was now leading by three metres, striding towards the water jump. Katya pushed through the last level of pain, forcing her feet to close on the heels of her rival. At the water jump, both landed one foot atop the barrier, both feet in the water. Still Shannon led, now by five metres. Katya pressed as they met the hurdle in the finishing straight. Shannon checked, right foot leading, clambering clumsily over the obstacle. Katya, four strides behind, pressed, lifted by Shannon's hesitation at the barrier; perhaps she had no more. Katya now endured a level of pain she had never before experienced, the suffering that comes only rarely when champion meets champion. Through she ran, no quarter to the screams from her body, a cacophony of nerve ends beseeching her brain and muscles to cease strangling her bones.

She heard the school bell ring as they started the final lap. Katya, lengthened her stride, ran to meet Sylvia Mietl, the balls of her feet bruised as they drove against the track, sucking in air, searing the passage to her lungs, over the first hurdle, over the second, over the third, through the water towards the final hurdle, both athletes matching strides, hearts pounding now at close to four beats per second. Side by side they raced.

Katya's instinct spoke to her quietly, calmly, "Do it . . . do it." She listened and drove her right foot into the track before the hurdle. Katya could see the hurdle five strides in front. Four . . . . . . three . . . . . . two and a half strides, her eyes said. She needed to check . . . . . . One and a half strides . . . . . . She stretched her legs as never before. She cleared the top with her left foot, pulled her right foot over as the left bit into the track. Shannon jerked her legs over the top of the hurdle to follow, four metres behind as they raced down the home straight towards the tape, stretched across the track at chest height.

As Katya ran toward the tape, she now knew; her quest was fulfilled. Five metres from the tape she ran inside the track, she ran inside the finish line.

Shannon Myers burst through the tape, the new Olympic Champion. Ileana Donat of Romania finished second and Sudha Lall, in third place, won India's first female track medal.

A heartbeat of silence quieted the stadium as Katya jogged towards the tunnel. Then, a tsunami of sound crashed about her. She smiled a Mona Lisa, questions answered, no need to ever ask again.

THE END

Also by Larry Tracey

"Seagulls Dance"

Read the first chapter

Chapter 1

THE Irish village of Corryann, the First of September, 1794.

Connor Macken lay gazing at the sky, the white seagulls above dancing against the azure canvas in time with nature's orchestra. The scent of his wife Kathleen and the freshly crushed grass mingled with the salty taste of the air. The fingertips of Connor's right hand gently tickled the small hairs on the nape of Kathleen's neck. Her slender fingers were at once pressing and pulling the button on her blouse 'til her modesty was recovered.

Absorbed in contemplation, Connor lay some six paces from the cliff's edge, his back compressing the turf beneath him. The soles of his bare feet pressed down upon the grass, his breeches re-fastened at the waist by a knotted leather belt. He wore no shirt; this garment lay squashed beneath his head allowing his eyes to gaze through his toes at the headland and the sea beyond. The sunlight warmed his chest and face, minute droplets of water gathering on his torso like early morning dew. It was certain from his complexion and exposed toes that the sun had, for many summers, bathed him in its warmth. Connor's eyelids were slipping, resting on the brown lashes beneath. His mind was massaged by the steady rhythmic shush of the waves caressing the sand on the beach below. The intermittent whisper of the wind traversed the nearby field of ripened corn. The cymbals clashed from the ocean as the waves from the sea battered the rocks impeding their progress. Recollections of the past floated leisurely, impassively cerebral.

It was six years to the day since Kathleen and he had pledged themselves to each other before the villagers of Corryann. The images of that time, his feelings as he walked to the small church remained fresh in his head even today, especially today...It had been his nineteenth birthday. His feet, as he strode out towards the church were inhibited by the novelty of wearing boots which he'd borrowed for the occasion; his heart swelled, pressing out his chest against the freshly laundered, grey, collarless shirt. Cock of the village he felt as he led his three friends towards his matrimony, David and Mark jostling him, Mark's foot set out to trip him. The yell when Connor's boot made contact with his ankle brought smiles and grins from the others as Mark hopped on one leg, clasping the suffering ankle as if to stop the pain escaping, his upper teeth exposed, gripping his lower lip to contain his anguish.

"You'll not be wearing the boots in a few hours. It'll be her who'll be doing the kicking," laughed David.

"Not just the boots, she'll have your trousers too," quipped Mark releasing his ankle. "She's a fine spirited woman is Kathleen. She'll be sure to have the measure of you," he continued, his face contorted now in glee at his own wit.

"Pay no heed to them," Christopher, the third and closest of his friends rejoined. "You're the best match for each other there ever was," he concluded in support of Kathleen and Connor.

Connor nodded in agreement at his best friend's wise words. Wasn't he the luckiest of men to have a girl such as Kathleen love him above all other suitors? Indeed, love him so much that she was prepared to marry him, live out the rest of their lives in each other's company. For sure, the date, the first of September, would forever after be a special day in his calendar.

Connor remembered they were the first to arrive at the church. His friends had tried to persuade him to tarry longer at the inn, to slake his thirst with a tankard of ale they beguiled but the only thirst that he had that day, was to be married to Kathleen. His friends understood.

"It's through no fault of your own," consoled David. "It's a sickness you have and ale's not the remedy," he smirked.

"Women seem to have that effect on some fellows," rejoined Mark, winking at David. "Thank God it's not contagious."

With nearly an hour to go before the ceremony, Connor pushed on the heavy, wooden door. He entered the church, the stillness inside calming his pulsing heart. His three friends stayed outside in the sunshine, "to give you time alone to re-think this folly," joked David, addressing Connor's back.

Sitting in the first right-hand pew available for common folk, Connor was five benches from the altar. All seats in front were marked with the name of the local notable who had bought the right to sit closer to God. Connor bade his mind ignore the slight for he knew none of the notables were likely to attend this day.

The thought of those who would not witness his day caused tears to well from his eyes, streaking the day's dust on his face, dripping from his chin to wet his clasped hands. No, Sarah Macken, his mother, she had gone to God before Connor's sixth birthday. She died soon after the birth of his sister Veronica, herself an angel within two days. They lay buried together outside this church. Connor prayed hard to God that they could see him now. His body ached that they should share his joy. Gerard Macken, his father, sailed to Spain to fight for the coin, driven to leave Corryann for the crops had been poor for two seasons. Landlord's rent and churchman's tithes were still payable on pain of eviction from land and home. He remained like so many other young men of Ireland, finished on a foreign field in search of a means to live on their own land. It was five years since the tidings of his death. Connor's sadness increased by the lack of a grave to mourn over. His hands now clasped so tight in prayer, his knuckles seemed close to breaking through the skin. The effort of prayer quelled Connor's aching. Comfort came from his belief that his family would be looking down with pride when Kathleen and he pledged each to the other.

Kathleen...ah...Kathleen...melancholy melted from Connor's mind at the thought of her. In a short while she'd be beside him. They had known each other all their lives save for the fact that Connor was eighteen months the elder. For the past fifteen months and three days they had been walking out together. It was nine months to the day since Connor had called on Seamus McDonagh, Kathleen's uncle and guardian. Seamus' consent was willingly given. Connor had then undertaken all manner of tasks from dawn 'til well past dusk to gather the five shillings required by the local churchman, Fitzpatrick, for the wedding.

Christopher, a broad grin on his face, had knelt beside Connor, touching his arm with a gentle squeeze of encouragement, Connor returning his smile. Shuffling noises came from behind as the villagers arrived. He awaited Kathleen, his stomach tightening, his mouth parched – what if she'd changed her mind? Then Kathleen was beside him, standing, talking, Fitzpatrick, Seamus, Christopher, villagers smiling, the bright sunlight, as he walked out of the church, Mrs Kathleen Macken on his arm. For all he tried, Connor could not replay the church ceremony in his mind. All that went before, most of what came after, were clear in his memory, the event itself presenting only abstract imagery in his head.

"What amuses you so?" asked Kathleen, tickling Connor's left nostril with a blade of grass.

Connor awakened from his reverie and, itching the spot with the knuckle of his forefinger, replied, "I was reliving our wedding day." He rolled over, pinning Kathleen to the ground.

"And I'll bet I know which part of the day made you smile so," she wheezed with the weight upon her, twinkling blue eyes signalling her own interpretation.

"Is it more you're after, you wanton woman?" rejoined Connor, "For if it is, I'm the man for it!" His lips closed in on hers.

As the passion of the embrace hardened, Kathleen rolled, pushing Connor onto his back, she now atop, astride his stomach.

"We've our son, Liam, to go to!" she mockingly admonished. "There's been enough babymaking for one day. We've to tend to the one we already have. Yomi will expect us to collect him soon," she said as she pushed her palms against his chest to regain her feet.

"It's for the want of a daughter that I put my body through all this strain," laughed Connor as he rose to his feet, plucking his shirt from the turf.

Kathleen and Connor stood facing the blue of the sea, his left arm thrown across her shoulders, her right arm about his waist, her hand resting upon his hip.

"What a wondrous place it is," sighed Kathleen.

"We surely have been blessed," replied Connor as his eyes followed the line of seaweed meandering along the sand below, the warmth of the sun drying patches from black to bottle green. The vivid, golden colour of the sand below the straggling seaweed path lay in contrast with the dusty fawn of the shore above the tideline.

"Look at the way the sea makes its lather," he pointed out to Kathleen as bubbles of air at the water's edge fought to escape the embrace of the sea, only to be recaptured as fresh waves broke upon the shore in the rhythmic ocean flow.

"That's not much of a lather!" Kathleen retorted. "Sure, look at the ocean there, now. That's a lather!" she stated, turning her gaze to her left. Connor followed her eyes. A fine mist of salty dew bathed their faces. He nodded in agreement. A few paces to their left, the cliff face had subsided. Some sixty feet below, the wreckage was strewn across the beach, tumbling into the sea. The ocean, in defence of its territorial rights, sent waves crashing, clashing with the obstinate rocks too large to dislodge, creating a spray of brine carried ashore on the breeze.

"This is my favourite place in the whole of Corryann," said Kathleen. "It's here that I listen to the messages from the sea, hark the tales of the gulls above." She breathed deeply, "In times of trouble and moments of joy, I find solace here," she concluded, looking into Connor's eyes. Connor's brown eyes locked onto Kathleen in support of her words.

"I don't understand why but I do know what you mean."

The sun was close to touching the ocean on the horizon as they turned from the headland. They paused. Sails of a ship had gathered their attention. Some eight miles distant, it entered Clay harbour.

"I wonder if it's bringing in new cotton?" queried Kathleen. "The last time I went to Clay there was little to be had," she said.

"We can go to Clay in a few weeks, once harvesting has finished," Connor replied as they turned towards their cottage and the village of Corryann some one mile distant.

Kathleen playfully pushed Connor who, unbalanced, landed on the seat of his trousers. She ran giggling at the mischief she had caused. It was some four hundred yards down the track before Kathleen's laughter was cut short, replaced by a girlish shriek as Connor caught her by the waist. They were now alongside the ripened fields of corn which covered much of the ground between themselves and the village. The two-acre field to their right was their crop, the land rented, as was their cottage, from the cleric, Fitzpatrick.

"It's a fine harvest," said Connor still holding Kathleen by the waist as they stopped to survey the ripened ears. "There will be enough to provide food 'til this time next year," he continued.

"Even after we've paid Fitzpatrick his rent and church tithes?" interrupted Kathleen.

"For sure, for sure. Some of our obligations are already met from my unpaid labour on his land," Connor stated emphatically, aware of his wife's concern.

Moving his hands from her waist to hold her hands, Connor stared intently into Kathleen's face, "This I promise you Kathleen, we will never want for food, not you, not Liam, not any of us. I will always stay here beside you to provide for you, I swear. I'll never be driven to leave for the want of coin," he promised. Kathleen squeezed his fingers between her own in acceptance of his words.

Hands clasped, they continued down the track that led to their one-roomed cottage on the outskirts of Corryann.